SUPERBIKE

David Allen Russell

David Allen Russell
5/26/93

High Octane Productions, Inc.
Laguna Beach, CA 92651

FIRST EDITION

Library of Congress Catalogue in Publication Data

Russell, David Allen
Superbike

Summary: A shy 12 year old named Bernard Wheel, who lives in a foster home, has built his own mountain bike out of discarded parts. He calls it SUPERBIKE and rides it throughout the hills and forests near his home with his pet parrot, Mr. Birdy, on his shoulder. Bernard plays soccer with the Blue Angels, who are competing for the state championship against a rival team made up of a gang of bullies and ruffians from a neighboring town.

[1. Orphans - Fiction. 2. Soccer - fiction 3. Bicycles - Fiction]
93-77390
ISBN: 1-883174-00-7

Published by High Octane Productions, Inc.

Printed in the United States of America

This novel is dedicated to my son Mark, and to my daughters Sarah, Michelle, Susan and Elaina, and to all of the boys and girls of the world who have loved their bikes.

PROLOGUE

When you are a newspaper reporter as I am, you can run across some pretty strange stories sometimes, and they usually come along just when you least expect it. Sometimes they are so strange and outrageous that you can't even put them in print. Some you forget right after writing them, and some you remember for a long time, and maybe once in a lifetime, there is a story that grabs you so hard that you never can forget it. Well, in my long and illustrious career, there is just one special story that I think of almost every day. Perhaps it is because of the mystery surrounding it, maybe because I could never figure it out, I don't really know. I only know that it is one that haunts me, and one that I will never forget for as long as I live.

I was doing investigative reporting for the Flagstaff News way back in the year 1989, writing just about everything from automobile accidents to politics, but mostly police and crime stuff. Then one day Big Jim Muldoon, my editor, called me in and told me that he needed me to do a story on a sports event. "Sports?" I said. "I don't know very much at all about sports," and he said, "I know that, but my regular sports reporter is out sick and this is a really big event for our area so I need you to do it. You can give it some kind of a twist in your own style, if you want to."

Well, when he said that, I had no idea what a really big twist this story was going to have, so I just sort of yawned and said, "Okay boss. I'll do my best, but I'm no sports reporter."

So, what choice did I have anyway? They paid my salary and treated me well. The boss raised an eyebrow and shot a look of disdain at me, so I continued with, "Okay, what is this big event?"

"It's the International Mountain Bike Race," he said, "and all the champion mountain bike racers from all over the world will be right here in Flagstaff to compete for the grand prize."

"I never even heard of it," I told him, "but it sounds interesting. When does it start?"

He gave me all the information, telling me that it was in the mountains near Sedona, just South of Flagstaff, and that it was scheduled to begin that coming Saturday. Then he handed me an envelope with $300.00 in cash and a credit card in it and told me that there was a room reserved for me in the Desert Pines Resort, a big expensive and classy place where only rich people stayed. "You take the rest of the week and the weekend," he said. "Have yourself a little vacation. Anything else you need you can charge on the hotel bill."

"Great," I said, pocketing the envelope.

"Write the story. Cover every part of it. Stress the human aspect and get all the details of the race for the readers who don't understand it. Get us interviews with all the championship riders before the race, some photos, and cover the whole event. The usual stuff, you know."

Well, it looked just like a piece of cake to me. A walk in the woods, and a paid holiday to boot, so I patted my pocket to make sure the envelope was still there, shook his hand, went home and packed a small bag, then took off down the highway for Sedona.

The interviews with the bikers were all good, and I enjoyed all the people, and wrote my usual stuff about it, then came the day of the race, and the biggest surprise that I ever had in my life.

The racers were all lined up behind this big yellow starting ribbon, all decked out in their colorful riding suits, on these fabulous special mountain bikes. The crowd was big, with at least five thousand people watching. Then the starting gun went off, the ribbon dropped, and they all started off together; the best riders in the world all competing for that big grand prize and the title of the best rider in the world. Then, about fifty yards down the trail, there was a kind of moan from the crowd, and some people were pointing up at the side of the hill to the trees above and behind the racers. I shaded my eyes from the hot sun, scanned the trees, and then I saw this kid on a bike barreling down the side of the mountain in a cloud of dust. He was all dressed in blue, and he was riding this weird looking red and silver bike, and he was wearing a blue kind of motorcycle helmet with a dark visor so that we couldn't see what he looked like. Anyway, he rode down off the mountain, fell in behind these championship riders about a hundred yards back, and within ten or fifteen seconds he had caught up with and passed each an every one of them. It was amazing, and he continued to ride ahead of them throughout the race as if daring them to catch him. Once in a while someone would get close, and then he would just put on more speed, putting a comfortable distance between him and the first of the championship riders. The race went on for twenty seven miles over rough terrain, through trees, over rocks, up and down hills, through little streams and he led the pack all the way to the finish line. Just before the yellow ribbon was a kind of hump in the trail, and this kid hit that bump and he and that strange looking bike took right off into the air. He flew like a bird right over that yellow ribbon and soared farther than I have ever seen anyone jump any car or motorcycle, much less a bike, and then came down and did a giant wheeley, before disappearing into the trees at the end of the trail. Of course there was a regular winner of the race, one of those champions who entered and rode the race according to all the rules, and everyone agreed that the rules stated that you had to break the ribbon instead of jumping over it, but the performance of this kid had all the news people talking mostly about him, and that kind of took the pleasure out of winning for the real winner, especially since the kid had outshone them all with his dazzling speed and that fantastic jump. I guess I don't need to tell you that this turned out to be a very big story for me and for all of the news media people. We all tried everything we knew to find out who this kid was, but in the end we came up against a brick wall and we were never able to. To this day it remains a big mystery. One of the TV stations even offered a ten thousand dollar reward for information that would help us find out who this kid was, but that didn't work either. Even though this was five years ago, I still go out to all the little towns around Sedona every year on my vacation and ask questions of everyone that I can, hoping to find the answer, but so far it has been a complete dead end. I thought I had some clues from time to time, but none of them ever panned out, and as far as I know this mysterious bike rider never entered any other race like that again, unless he did it the regular way. So we never did find out who this kid was. That is the reason that in every newspaper or magazine story that you read, or whenever you see a story about this incident on television, the kid in the blue suit and helmet, with that strange looking red and silver bike is just referred to as, SUPERBIKE.

Jack Prescott
THE FLAGSTAFF NEWS

CHAPTER ONE

(Five years earlier. Somewhere in Arizona)

Bernard knew that he had a very unusual name. It was the kind of name that made people's eyes get real wide the very first time that they heard it, and they would say the name back to him with a question mark at the end of the sentence. "Bernard Wheel?" they would say. "What an unusual name." And then Bernard would tell them that he had picked the name out himself. That was one of the good parts about being found in a basket on the steps of Mrs. Mueller's foster home when he was just a baby.

They had just called him Little Guy until he was old enough. Then Mrs. Mueller, who ran the foster home, and was like a mom to him, had let him pick out his own name, and Bernard had picked Bernard Wheel. He liked the name Bernard, because of a movie that he had seen on

TV about those big Saint Bernard dogs that rescued people who got lost in the snow, and he liked the name Wheel as a last name because of the new trail bike that Mrs. Mueller had given him on his twelfth year at the home. Well, it wasn't exactly a new bike. It had been made out of parts of some other bikes that were so old and broken that they had been discarded, and Mrs. Mueller and Mr. Brown, his teacher from school, had collected all the good parts, fixed them, painted them, and assembled them into a bike that looked as if it was better than brand new, and given it to him for Christmas.

Bernard had worked on the bike too. Just as soon as he got it, he had learned all about taking it apart and putting it back together, just like a giant jigsaw puzzle. Then, he had added parts of his own, re-made the whole bike, and tinkered with it until it was faster than any bike around, and he had made it real rugged too so that he could ride it out in the hills and on the trails in the countryside that surrounded the little town of Miners Oaks. The bike was very special to Bernard, and Bernard called it his "Superbike." And when he was through getting it as mechanically perfect as he possibly could, he re-painted it and would shine and polish it every day until it was the most beautiful bike in the whole town of Miners Oaks. Maybe, even in the whole state of Arizona.

Just this last Saturday afternoon, a week ago, Bernard had installed a mirror that had been given to him by Joe Duffy, the mechanic at the corner gas station. He was out in the garage, wiping the last bit of wax off and shining it until he could see his face in the chrome part. It was funny the way the curve of the metal distorted the light, bending his nose and making his cheeks seem twice as round and freckled as they actually were. He poked out his tongue and laughed out loud at the way it looked in the distorted reflection, like a long pink snake. He wiggled the tip of it and watched it change shapes in the convex shape of the chrome. It sure was funny. Bernard tried grabbing both his ears, pulled them straight out, crossed his eyes, then wiggled his tongue. That one was so funny that he rolled over backwards on the floor and laughed out loud. Suddenly his laughter was interrupted by the sound of Mrs. Mueller's musical voice singing to him from the house. "Bernard, it's time for soccer practice."

Bernard choked on the last bit of his laugh, stifled a giggle, got to his feet, brushed the hay from his sweater and went to the door of the garage to answer. "All right, Mrs. Mueller," he said. "I'll be ready in just a minute."

"Well, hurry up or you'll be late," Mrs. Mueller sang back. "You spend far too much time daydreaming and fiddling with that bike of yours."

"Coming, Mrs. Mueller," Bernard called back from the doorway, then he carefully wiped his tools clean and put them all neatly back in their proper places. The big silver crescent wrench was something that Mrs. Mueller had given him and he used it the most so he hung that on the nail above his tool bench where he could get it easily and see it all the time. The little socket set that he had bought with his lunch money one day on the way home from school he put in the drawer. The screwdrivers were hung neatly in order on the pegboard on the wall, the smallest ones on the left and the biggest ones on the right, with the Phillips screwdrivers all hung below them in the same order. Bernard stepped back to see how neat everything looked, then he closed the door of the garage and walked across the back lawn to the porch at the rear of the house to wash his hands.

There was a song running around in Bernard's mind as he lathered up. It was a melody that he couldn't get out of his head. Familiar and yet elusive, and as he scrubbed he did it to the tempo of that song, humming along with it. The soap was that kind that smelled real good like regular soap, but it had gritty stuff in it like sand or something to help scrape all the grease off. Mrs. Mueller had bought that kind of soap especially for him because he was the only one in the house who got really dirty hands. "Boys are like that," Mrs. Mueller would say, as she passed the peas and the potatoes and gravy at dinner time, and Bernard would blush when she talked about him. "Boys will be boys, and they get much dirtier than girls." Then she would give him a loving pat and a kiss on the cheek to let him know that it didn't bother her any that boys got dirty. Mrs. Mueller was a neat lady and although she wasn't Bernard's real mother, she was certainly the next best thing to it. Maybe even better, Bernard thought, because he didn't really know what his real mom might be like. Maybe she would not even be as good a mom as Mrs. Mueller. After all, Bernard knew for certain that Mrs. Mueller would never leave him on a porch in a basket on a cold winter night.

From the time that he had been left on her doorstep many years ago, she had been the only mother Bernard had ever known. She had been there through all his sicknesses as well as in the good times, and although Little Mary and Jerry and Veronica lived in the foster home too, she had always devoted time to Bernard whenever he needed it. She was a strict woman when it came to discipline, but very fair and really understanding. Perhaps that was because of her own unhappy childhood. She had lost both her parents in World War Two, then her uncle had taken her and escaped from Hungary to Spain, then got a job in South America. After a few years he brought her to the United States, where he got a job as a miner but he had passed away shortly after coming to Miners Oaks, and Mrs. Mueller had been raised in several foster homes herself. Married when she was very young, her husband had been drafted, then reported missing in action in the Vietnam war. Although Mrs. Mueller always hoped that he would someday be found, and waited patiently, he was never heard from again. So Mrs. Mueller, childless and alone, vowed never again to marry, but instead to devote herself to raising homeless kids, and she was doing a good job of it.

"Don't forget your knee pads and soccer shoes," Mrs. Mueller said, popping into the back porch and thrusting them into Bernard's just-dried hands. "Supper is at seven so don't be late."

"Okay," Bernard said. She grabbed his arm, gave him a little kiss on the cheek and a pat on his backside, then standing upright, she flashed a big smile on him and blew him a kiss before turning and going back into the kitchen. It was an electrifying smile that made him feel warm all over. He knew that Mrs. Mueller really loved him, and that felt really good.

That song was still running around in Bernard's mind as he went out the back door. It was a melody that he couldn't get out of his head, and as he took Superbike out of the garage and locked the door, he began to hum the tune out loud to himself. A bird in a nearby tree whistled along.

Strapping his pads and shoes to the back of Superbike with a stretchy bungy cord, Bernard checked it by pulling it way back then letting it go to make sure it was plenty tight. "Kawhack!" it went. "Kawack yourself," Bernard said in time to the music, then he put his leg over Superbike and sat on the saddle.

From a pocket in his belt-wallet he withdrew the stopwatch that he had earned by mowing Sheriff George's lawn six Sundays in a row this last summer. He polished the shiny silvery metal case on his pants leg, then popped open the lid and punched the button setting the timer in motion. Quickly then, he closed the lid, slipped it back into its denim belt-wallet pocket, jumped up in the air and came down hard on the pedal. The rear wheel spun as he and Superbike leapt forward, spewing a trail of dirt and dust out behind as they raced together out of the yard and up the pathway toward the hills.

That song was blasting in Bernard's head. A roaring base line, drums hitting a heavy beat, and high guitars wailing away. He shifted gears at the bottom of Big Rock Pass and pedaled to the rhythm, driving each pedal push hard and deep, making Superbike take wings. The strong, thick vibrations of the music filled him with a power that he directed from his mind to the pedal, making Superbike fly up the trail. Through the trees he raced, toward the sharp turn at Blueberry Ridge, then down the equestrian path through Candy Canyon. Gaining more speed with every turn of the wheel, Bernard shifted into another gear as he passed the big petrified oak called Hangman's Tree and Superbike took off like a rocket.

Reaching the very crest of the ridge at Overlook Bluff, Bernard pulled the front wheel up into the air and held it there, balancing on the back wheel and making a complete turn around before letting it down and starting down the other side of the mountain toward Prairie Dog Meadow. He held his head low over the handlebars to cut wind resistance, and, pushing Superbike ever harder, shifted up two more gears. The trees on either side of the path were transformed from individual entities into one green indiscernible blur. Bernard focused his attention upon a particular tree far ahead at the very bottom of the trail and held the handlebars hard to keep Superbike in a perfectly straight line. One mistake at this speed could spell disaster. Bernard knew that because in the past he had taken some pretty bad spills which had resulted in nasty cuts and bruises and some of them had taken a long time to heal. He thought of that now. Remembering the pain. Vowing not to let it happen again as he went faster, and faster, and faster.

Torrents of whistling wind roared around him, slashing and whipping at his face, and his jacket filled with a pocket of air and billowed out around his back. Bernard gently pushed the gear lever forward. Seventh gear, eighth, ninth, tenth gear, skipping then to fifteenth, then as his ability to move his legs any faster diminished, he popped it all the way into 21st. Top gear. He was flying. It was awesome. He seemed to be standing still in a vacuum as the rest of the world turned. Almost at the bottom of the hill. He was topping out now, full speed, rocketing down the trail like a bullet from a rifle. It was a moment of absolute perfection, pure joy. Fun. "Wheeeeeeeeee!"

Then, there was a slight bump as the front tire hit a pothole in the trail. Superbike shuddered, but Bernard hung on and didn't lose it. The trail started to level out along the side of Prairie Dog Meadow, but up ahead was a slight rise, a bump, a kind of mogul. Bernard steadied for it, pumping hard with one last burst of energy before hitting the sharp rise. The bike suddenly bumped, then went upward at a thirty five degree angle. Bernard straightened up in the saddle, lifted himself on the pedals, pulled gently back on the handlebars. The front wheel went over the top and out into the air, then the back wheel left the ground and Bernard and Superbike were airborne. They soared out into the silent blue of the afternoon sky as if in slow motion, as if they were suspended in time, as if they would never come down, it was wonderful, and it seemed that it would just keep going on forever. On, and on, and on, and on....

But just when Bernard thought, and hoped, that it might never end, that he could just fly out into the sky and keep on going forever, the rear wheel came gently into contact with the trail. There was a squeak of rubber and a tiny puff of smoke from the tire as it met the unyielding ground. It spun from a dead stop to full rotation, then Bernard slid quickly back on the seat, and holding back on the handlebars and balancing Superbike on the rear wheel, he rode on down the trail, and clear to the end of the meadow in one long and glorious wheely.

The bike path around Lake Madera Azul was level and paved so when the front wheel finally came down, Bernard just let Superbike coast. He leaned casually back, locked his hands behind his head, relaxed as though he were in the hammock that hung on the front porch at home, and let Superbike glide all the way past the Lake Madera Azul, through the forest, past Palmer's Pines, the old Indian caves, and all the way to the Miners Oaks Elementary School. It was really neat.

The Blue Angels were already practicing out on the field as Bernard rolled up the driveway, zoomed past the baseball diamond and the gymnasium, coasted up the gravel drive, and then turned sideways making a perfect sliding stop at the bike racks.

Locking Superbike carefully in, Bernard quickly got his stopwatch out and pushed the button. "Gosh," he muttered to himself, "Twelve minutes and thirty four seconds. That's thirty two seconds better than I've ever done it before."

"Come on, Bernard," he heard Coach Bob yell from the middle of the playing field. "You're late again." The coach tapped at the face of his wristwatch and waggled a finger at Bernard to emphasize his point, and show his disapproval. Bernard was embarrassed.

"I'm coming, Coach," he yelled back, then jogged out onto the field to join his team.

"You're one of my best players, Bernard," Coach

Bob said, "but you have to learn to be on time. It's very important to be on time. I shouldn't have to tell you that. If you are late once more, you don't get to play in the first quarter at the biggest and most important game of the year. Those are the rules, and they are the same for you as they are for everybody."

"I'm sorry, Coach, "Bernard said. "I was waxing my bike, and I guess I just took a little too long."

"It's great to have a shiny bike Bernard, but they don't allow you to ride them in soccer games."

"I know, coach."

What we need to do now is practice. Practice, practice, and more practice, because that's the only way you ever get good at anything. Now get out there and kick some balls around with Turtle and Ernie, and Jojo. I want you guys to practice that four-way pass technique and the hide-the-ball routine I showed you last week. Okay?"

"Okay, Coach."

There was a loud "Pong." Bernard knew that sound. It was the sound a soccer ball made when you kicked it real hard and made perfect contact. Kind of like a gun shot, but with a mellow musical echo after it for a split second. As though that sound was trapped inside the air-filled center of the ball. He turned his head quickly to see Ernie running toward him with a big smile on his face. The ball was in the air between them, and heading right at Bernard's head. He bent his knees and pulled his head down and "SWISH" the ball zoomed over like a cannon shot. Bernard turned his head and saw Turtle catch it on his forehead and butt it back toward Jojo, then Jojo kicked it to Bernard. "You gonna practice, or just stand there like a nerd?" Turtle said as he zoomed by.

"Sure," Bernard said catching the ball with both hands.

"You trying to bean me, or something?" Bernard dropped the ball to his toe and kicked it back to Ernie.

"I knew you'd duck," Ernie said, out of breath. "Quack, quack. Quaaak! Get it? duck..."

Ernie was a little bigger than Bernard, with skin the color of chocolate and black wavy hair. He was just an inch or so taller than Bernard but a whole lot thicker in the body, and more muscular than any of the other boys. Actually, all of the boys in Bernard's class were a little bigger than he was, and Bernard sometimes wondered why he didn't seem to grow, even though he got older. Ernie was his best friend. He was always making jokes and wisecracks about everything. "I get it," Bernard said. "Yuk, yuk, yuk."

Turtle was a lot thicker in the body. Actually, he was wide enough to be divided into two boys the size of Bernard and Ernie and have some left over, but he could really move around the soccer field. He ran over now. "Pass the ball," he yelled.

"Why don't you just play with this?" Ernie quipped, poking Turtle in his pot belly. "It's big and round like a soccer ball."

"That's my lunch," Turtle said. "Don't mess with it."

"At least you don't have to worry about falling down. You'd just roll."

"I keep this just in case we ever get lost in the forest," Turtle said. "You guys would both die of starvation and I'll still have half a tank."

"Yeah? You look like a tank," Ernie quipped.

"Let's practice," Jojo said. He was always the serious one, only joking occasionally, and when he did his white teeth shone bright against his dark Apache skin and coal black hair. "Coach wants us to practice the hide-the-ball routine, so let's do it."

"Jojo is right," Bernard put in, taking the ball and

spinning and balancing it on one finger. "We can't get better if we don't practice, practice, practice."

Ernie grabbed the ball, dropped it on the ground and kicked it across to Turtle. "Let's go," he said, and they all took off running down the field. Near the goal the ball was quickly passed to Turtle, who passed it over to Bernard, who passed it to Ernie, who passed it back to Turtle. "Go, go, go," Turtle called out, then he and Ernie took off in one direction passing the ball back and forth between them while Bernard ran way over to the side of the playing field. They were far apart now, Turtle and Ernie together and Bernard alone, then Turtle and Ernie moved around and around each other, hiding and passing the ball fast, making it almost impossible to follow the action with the eye, while Jojo ran off to the other side.

Bernard was in position and Ernie suddenly punched the ball way over to the side where Jojo was, and Jojo kicked it to Bernard so fast that the ball was a blur, and Bernard banged it into the goal net. "Very good," coach Bob yelled from way down the field. "Now do it a hundred more times."

"The coach is a slave driver," Ernie quipped.

"And we are the slaves," Turtle said.

"Yeah, but he's the best darned coach in Arizona," Bernard said, "and if we're gonna beat the Green Hornets next Sunday, we'd better listen to what he has to teach us."

"I'd rather be playing cowboys and Indians," Turtle said.

"Can I be a cowboy?" Jojo asked, grinning broadly, grabbing the ball, then kicking it up the field. Then, he took off after it, with Turtle, Ernie, and Bernard running right after him.

CHAPTER TWO

The afternoon sunlight glittered upon the shiny glass surface of the binoculars that J.D. Turpole held, sending a flash of reflected light bouncing down toward the playing field, but the Blue Angels were all concentrating hard upon their practice session, and not one of them noticed. If they had, they would certainly have been surprised to know that some of the bad boys from the Green Hornets team were watching their every move.

"That Bernard Wheel can really boot the soccer ball," J.D. said to Spider Kramer. "We have to find a way to keep him out of the game next Sunday."

"Maybe we should just wait until he starts for home, follow him, and stomp the stuffing out of him."

"Yeah," Ugly Joe said. "We could break his arms and legs. That would keep him out of the game, for sure."

The other boys in the gang all laughed at this idea,

but J.D., their elected leader, waved his hand at them and let out a hissing noise to quiet the gang all down. "Shhhhh!," he said in a raspy whisper. "You want them to know that we are here? How can we learn their soccer moves if we can't keep this a secret?"

"Yeah. Keep quiet you guys," Spider said, trying to pass the buck.

"And that means you too, Spider," J.D. said threateningly. "Shut up!"

"Sorry J.D. I just got a little excited at the thought of hurting that Bernard guy."

"Yeah, well we ain't gonna beat him up. That would just be a little too obvious. Besides it would blow our cover and then they'd probably call the whole game off."

"Aw, darn it," Wimp said. "I never thought of that."

"That's why I'm the leader and you are the follower," J.D. gloated. "You guys just let me do the thinking and everything will be O.K."

"Okay, boss, but how can we keep him out of the game if we don't bust him up?"

"Well, we might fix it so he has some kind of accident."

"Accident?" Spider asked. "What kind of accident?"

"Don't worry. I have a couple of ideas, and I'll tell you about them when the time comes. In the meantime, I don't want any of you guys shooting off your mouths about this and spilling the beans."

Spider rubbed his tummy and licked his lips. "Speaking of beans," he said, "I'm getting kinda hungry."

"O.K." J.D. said. "Let's cruise over to the hang-out; I don't think those Blue Angels can show us any moves that we don't already know. We can beat those guys with one hand tied behind us anyway, once that Bernard bimbo is out of the game."

"But you can't use your hands in soccer anyway, J.D.," Spider said.

"Shut up, Spider. Come on, guys, let's go." J.D. led the gang out of the bushes to their bikes, and on down the hill as the unsuspecting Blue Angels continued to practice on the school field far below.

Ernie took the ball down the field, ducked around Jojo who tried to intercept him, then passed it expertly to Bernard who kicked it sideways to Turtle, and Turtle smacked it into the net again. All the boys yelled with glee, except Jojo who pouted a bit at being suckered on the play. "Pretty tricky," Jojo said, trying to be a good sport about it even though his ego had been damaged a little bit. "Well, at least I'm glad that we're all on the same team."

"That was nothing," Turtle said. "You should see our butt-ball play."

"Butt-ball play?" Jojo said. "Never heard of a play like that."

"Me and Bernard and Turtle invented it," Ernie said proudly.

"When? I don't remember any play like that."

"A few weeks ago, when you had the flu," Turtle said boasting." Us cowboys were out roping steers while the Indians were home in their teepee."

"Wise guy. How does it work?" Jojo asked.

"Let's show it to him," Turtle said to Bernard.

Bernard turned and took a look up the field. One group of boys were practicing kicking goals, a good 75 yards away at the other net, and Coach Bob was supervising another group of boys practicing passing about half way up the field. Nobody was looking their way.

"This is just something we did on our own,"

Bernard said. "For fun. You know, the coach doesn't know about it, or anything. It's kind of a secret, and, you know, we're supposed to be practicing passing."

"Nobody's watching, Bernard," Turtle said. "Let's show him. Come on...real fast."

Ernie put the ball on the ground and gave it a little push with his toe. "Come on, Bernard," he said. "Let's do it."

Ernie and Turtle ran up the field passing the ball, then turned and ran back toward the net, then Ernie passed the ball to Bernard, and Bernard moved toward the side of the field with it. Quickly Turtle ran toward the net, then Bernard passed the ball back to Ernie. When Turtle got to center field, about ten feet in front of the net, Ernie kicked the ball back to Bernard, and Bernard ran with it, dribbling down the sideline. Turtle suddenly stopped center field, then bent over and grabbed his knees and stood motionless.

"SMACK," was the noise that the ball made as Bernard kicked it, then almost instantly, "WHACK," as it hit Turtle on the rump, then ricocheted directly into the center of the net.

"Wow," Jojo hollered, then laughed. "A perfect bank shot."

"But you have to promise not to tell the coach," Bernard said.

"But it's a great play," Jojo argued. "We could use it in the game on Sunday."

"Naw, the coach would get mad. Especially if we tried it and missed. You have to promise not to tell," Bernard insisted.

"O.K., I promise. Scout's honor, but it sure was a swell play, and a perfect shot. Perfect."

The shrill sound of Coach Bob's whistle blew then, and as the boys looked up the field toward him, they saw him waving them all to come in. The Blue Angels all ran to where he stood and gathered around.

"O.K., you guys," Coach Bob said when the boys were all there forming a tight circle. "You guys are coming along great, but I don't have to tell you that those Green Hornets are big boys. They are tough, they play hard, and they play dirty. We are going to have to play a very tight game and outsmart them," Coach Bob tapped at his forehead and turned all around so that all the boys could see him. "I repeat, outsmart them, use the old bean. And do any of you know why?"

"Because they are bigger than us?" one of the boys asked.

"That's right. They are bigger, but we will be smarter, and faster, and play the game better, and do you know why?"

"Practice," the boys all said together.

"That's right. Practice makes perfect, but not just any practice. Perfect practice makes perfect. And we are going to practice, and practice perfect until we are blue in the face because we are... what?"

"The Blue Angels," the boys cried out in unison.

"Who are we?" Coach yelled.

"Blue Angels," the team yelled with more enthusiasm.

"That's right. You see, I believe in you and I know you can do it. Because you guys are all smart, smarter than the Green Hornets, so go home, get a good dinner and a good night's sleep, and we will all meet here tomorrow and the next day, and the next, and practice, practice, practice. Practice every day until we have all the moves we need to win. Now, tell me what Blue Angels never do."

"We never give up," the boys all chanted together.

Coach Bob put his hands up to his ears and

cupped them, "What?" he shouted. "I can't hear you." Then the boys all took gigantic breaths and shouted out as loud as they possibly could. "We never give up, never give up, never give up, yeaaaaah!"

"That's better," Coach Bob said. "See you all here tomorrow at the same time."

The boys all broke ranks then, heading in various directions. Some of them walking, a few being picked up by their parents in automobiles, but most of them taking their bikes.

Bernard, Ernie, Turtle, and Jojo all walked together to the bike racks. "Gee whiz," Ernie remarked as they stopped by the rack. "You put a new seat on your bike, Bernard."

"Naw, I just re-upholstered it," Bernard said, taking his lock and chain off.

"Zowee," Jojo said. "It looks like brand new."

"Where did you get that material?" Turtle asked. I've never seen any stuff like that on a bike seat before."

"I found it in a trash can. Well, it wasn't actually IN a trash can. I was just riding along," Bernard explained, "when I saw this old couch beside the trash cans. It was all ripped and torn with the cotton sticking out and all, but the cushions had these absolutely perfect pieces on the back of it where the material was just like brand new, so I cut the good pieces all out, took them home, and re-upholstered my seat with some of it."

"How did you learn to do that re-upholstery stuff?" Ernie asked, running his hand back and forth over the seat.

"Mrs. Mueller says that you have to do with what you have, so I just tried it, and it turned out pretty good."

"I'll say," Turtle was rubbing his hand over the seat too. "It's so smooth and soft," he commented. "Just like a baby's skin."

"Is it leather?" Jojo asked. "Some leather feels like a baby's skin."

"Naw," Bernard said. "It's some kind of man-made stuff, but it feels and looks like something real."

"Well, it sure is a neat seat. I'd like to have a seat like that for my bike."

"I have some left over. Enough to do some more seats. Maybe we could do them all."

"Then we could be a club," Ernie said. "A bike club."

"That would be radical," Jojo said. "Real radical."

"What's the difference between a club and a gang?" Turtle asked.

"Is this another joke?" Ernie quipped.

"Naw, I was just wondering." Turtle mounted his bike and pulled up alongside the others. "Seems like they are kinda the same."

"A tribe is kinda like a gang or a club, but a tribe works together for everyone's benefit. I think a gang is when people get together to do bad stuff."

Bernard mounted his bike. "A club is like our team," he said. "Guys working together to get better at something."

"That's right," Turtle said. "We can be a bike club so we can be the best bike riders around, right?"

"What will we call ourselves?" Ernie said. "One Indian, one fatso, and the cowboys?"

"Cowboys and Indians," Turtle suggested.

"Indians and cowpokes." Jojo commented. Why should the cowboys always get their name first?

Bernard laughed. "He's right. Maybe we should put the Indian name first, after all this is Arizona and they were here first. "How about the Apaches and the Dudes?"

"Wait," Jojo yelled. I'm not an Apache. I'm a Navajo."

"How about, this," Bernard suggested. We'll race and the first one to the dunes gets to pick the name?

"I'll go for that," Ernie said.

"Me too," Turtle agreed. "C'mon, you guys, let's race to the dunes and do some bike jumping."

"Okay," Jojo said. "Come on, Bernard."

"Well, O.K., but just for a little while. I have some chores to do at home, and I've got to get back in time for supper or Mrs. Mueller will be mad. I already got chewed out twice today for being late."

"Last one to the top of the hill is a dirty cowboy!" Jojo yelled as he dug out.

"Hey!" Ernie yelled after him. "No fair." Then he and Turtle took off right after Jojo.

Bernard was the last to get his bike out of the rack and by the time he did, mounted Superbike and dug out after them, they were already half way up the pathway, out into the tall sweet smelling summer grass and headed for the dunes.

Jojo pumped with all his might, trying to hold the slender lead he had gained by starting early, but as they went up the pathway toward the crest of Woodpecker Bluff, Ernie was closing in on Turtle and Bernard was not far behind, and gaining on them. At the bridle path crossing, Jojo crossed safely, but Turtle and Ernie had to slow and swerve, to avoid running into a couple of people on horseback. The horses reared and bolted, but the riders managed to hold the animals in control as Ernie, Turtle, and then Bernard zoomed by at tremendous speed.

Ernie passed Turtle as they reached Prairie Dog Meadow and turned right toward the dunes. On this long level stretch Bernard gained on, then passed, Turtle. At the big Tree Campground Bernard passed Ernie, and by the time they reached the first dune at the top of the hill Bernard was neck in neck with Jojo. In one final blast of speed, Superbike roared forward, passing Jojo and opening up a space between them that was as long as a football field. At the finish line, he turned sideways, skidded to a stop and waited for them all to pull up. They were all out of breath and panting like dogs on a hot summer day by then, but not too tired to laugh out loud at all the fun they were having.

"Let's play jackrabbit," Ernie said.

"Hey, that's a great name for our club," Bernard said. "The Jack Rabbits."

"Yeah," Ernie yelled. "we're the Jack Rabbits. Watch us go." Then he ran his bike full speed up a dune and jumped out into the air. It was a short jump, but one that was really fun, and for an hour they all jumped their bikes, racing around and laughing out loud until the sun began to cast a rosy red glow upon the sand dunes, and long dark shadows began to creep across the land.

"Time for me to go," Bernard said, looking at his watch. "I'll see you guys at practice tomorrow."

"Aw, come on. Stay a little longer," Ernie pleaded.

"Nope." Bernard said. "A promise is a promise, and I promised Mrs. mueller I wouldn't be late." So saying he spun his wheel, spurting sand out behind in a shower of dust, and headed off down the trail in the direction of Miners Oaks alone.

CHAPTER THREE

Hiding on a high ridge not far away, J.D. and his gang of hoodlums watched and waited. "He's coming down the trail," Spider said and J.D. and the other boys peered over the edge of the cliff to see.

"Now," J.D. said, "we'll put that Bernard Wheel out of action for good."

"How are we going to do that?" Wimp asked.

"See this big boulder? It's balancing right over the bike path below, so when Bernard comes along this way on his way home, this boulder will accidentally slip off and 'Bonkos' Bernard will get squished like a bug."

"That boulder is pretty solid," Spider said. "I don't think it's going to fall."

"It will if we help it to fall," J.D. said giving Spider a dirty look.

"Oh," Spider said. "I get it. We're going to push it on him."

"Brilliant thinking, Spider. Come on guys, let's clear these small rocks from around the bottom so it will roll, then you guys push. I'll take this big tree limb and pry from this side."

J.D. jammed the tree limb under the bottom of the big boulder and, placing a smaller rock under the middle of it, he made a lever to pry on the rock. He pulled hard and the boulder rocked. "It's loose," Wimp said.

"Good," J.D. said. "Now, watch until Bernard is right under the cliff, Spider, then let me know and I'll pry, and you guys push, and we'll start a landslide that will get that Bernard for sure."

Bernard rode slowly along the path, enjoying the ride and the way the setting sun cast red shadows over the rocky landscape, not realizing that danger lurked on the cliffs just above.

"Here he comes," Spider said in a half whisper, and the gang all braced themselves to push on the big boulder. J.D. got his big lever in place, and they all waited for Spider's signal.

"He's almost under the cliff. O.K. NOW!"

The boys all grunted and strained at the boulder and it began to move slightly, as J.D. pulled at the tree limb with all his weight. Then "CRACK," went the limb as it broke in half, sending J.D. down on his rump with a heavy thud and a cloud of dust. The boulder rocked back and forth a few times, then J.D. got up to look over the edge of the cliff just in time to see Bernard Wheel riding off into the green forest with the sun setting behind it.

"He never even knew we were here," Spider said, dusting J.D. off with his cap.

"Shut up, Spider" J.D. snorted.

"We can get him later," Spider said.

"Right," J.D. said. "But tonight we have a date with a few cows. We have some time before that game. Plenty of time to get Bernard later. Come on, guys. Let's ride."

All the boys mounted their bikes and followed J.D. down the trail and into the forest.

The Cooper farm was nearby. Bernard rode right near it on his way home. Sometimes he would see old Farmer Cooper out hoeing his corn or feeding his cows when he passed, and he would wave and Mr. Cooper would stop whatever he was doing and wave back. Or he might see Mr. Cooper's granddaughter, Ginger, feeding the chickens, and she would gesture and smile as Bernard went by, but Bernard had never ever really talked with them or knew much about them. As he passed the farm on his way home this evening, he would have been absolutely shocked if he had known what J.D. and his gang of roughnecks had planned to do at the Cooper farm later that night.

Miners Oaks had been a boom town at the turn of the century. Silver had been discovered there by a pioneer by the name of Jeremiah Smith, and there were stories in the history books about all the famous people that had come to the town during its boom times and all the adventures that they had. But when the silver vein went dry, all those who had come just to find their fortunes deserted Miners Oaks and left the little town to die. Only the few of its citizens who actually thought of the place as their home remained, and now nearly a hundred years later it was populated by the grandsons and granddaughters of those early pioneers, plus a few folks who had come, liked it there and stayed on. The town itself hadn't changed much over the years, except that the hustle and bustle of the boom-town days were all gone, and it was just a crossroads on the way to somewhere else. A sleepy little western town that never grew up, a tiny speck in small print on the road map of the territory, boasting a population of just 845 residents. It was a place where the general store closed at 8 p.m. and most everybody went to bed by nine; a place where everybody knew everybody else; a place where people took the word "neighbor" seriously. There was virtually no crime in Miners Oaks so Sheriff George Smith, a big man with a ready smile and a huge handlebar mustache that he kept curled and waxed at the tips, and who was proud of the fact that he was the grandson of that Smith who discovered silver here 100 years ago, had a job that consisted mainly of settling arguments between friends, issuing fishing licenses, and finding lost dogs. This was a town where a Sheriff could be a friend, and that's the way the people of Miners Oaks liked it.

CHAPTER FOUR

Bernard rode down off of Hillside Trail, put Superbike away in the garage, locked the door, then went into the house just as the sun settled behind the jagged pinnacle of Purple Mountain. In one last goodbye, it cast red and gold streaks above the peaks and out into the sky in multi-colored rays, tinting all the clouds a fiery red. Then it sank suddenly, pulling all the colors down with it, leaving a darkening dusk, followed by the gradually deepening black of night. It was hours later that the moon rose high above the tall pine trees, a big yellow moon in which, if you looked closely enough, and squinted exactly so, you could almost make out the image of a smiling face. It was a bright and happy glow that illuminated the town, the forest, and the valley beyond where the Cooper farm lay snuggled comfortably against the base of Mystery Mine Hills.

In the pasture near the farmhouse, a dozen or so contented cows grazed lazily upon the sweet, green grass, which now glistened golden in the moonlight. The faint sound of music wafted upon the night air, coming from the Cooper farmhouse, which lay just beyond the pasture with its lighted windows glowing in the night like cat's eyes. In the distance, the sound of a far off coyote echoed among the hills and canyons of the Mesa Verde Mountains, and the heavy buzz of crickets filled the cottonwood trees.

One hungry calf nuzzled contentedly at its mother's teat, and mother, chewing on a luscious bit of vegetation, turned to give her baby a loving glance. Little did they realize that at this very moment, danger lurked just beyond the fringes of the meadow in the bushes near the trees.

The snap of a twig under Spider Kramer's foot could have given them all away, but no one heard it but J.D. Turpole, who turned angrily and shot a killer look at his sidekick. "Shhhhhh," he hissed, then waved at the rest of the boys to park their trail bikes and follow him, taking cover in the bushes overlooking the meadow.

Just as they got into position to watch from this hidden vantage point, one of the lights in the farmhouse suddenly went out. Spider got so excited at seeing it that he grabbed J.D.'s coat sleeve, tugging it until J.D. turned angrily to see what he wanted.

"What," he snarled.

Spider pointed anxiously at the house saying, "Hey, J.D. A light just went out. Look. Look. Look."

J.D. jerked his arm away from Spider's impertinent grasp, hissing hot breath at him in a raspy and angry tone that sounded more like a rattlesnake about to strike than any human voice. "Shhhhhhhhhhh. You dummy, Spider. Quiet! I can see the lights. You think I'm blind or something? I can also see that some of them are still on. Can't you see that?"

"Aw, gee J.D. I want to get that cow so bad."

J.D. grabbed Spider by the jacket lapels and pulled him so close that they were nose to nose, then in that raspy and threatening whisper said, "I want to get the cow too, stupid. But not until I say so, and that will be after all the lights are out. You got that?"

So saying, he pushed Spider back so that Spider fell in a sitting position in the bushes. Crunch!

"O.K.," Spider sighed. "You're the boss."

"That's right. I am the boss. And don't you ever forget it."

All five of the boys settled down in the bushes to wait at J.D's order. Wimp and Ugly Joe slumped against a tree. Creep hung his lanky frame over a downed log, while J.D. took up a position behind some bushes to watch. Spider sat against a tree near him. After a while a few more of the lights in the farmhouse began to go out, but Spider yawned with impatience. His head began to droop, and he was sound asleep when the last of the lights went out. Ugly Joe was the first to notice. He made a whistle like a bird, but that didn't get Spider's attention, so he reached over and tapped him on the shoulder. Spider jumped in surprise when Joe's hand touched him unexpectedly from the dark. He rubbed his eyes until Joe came into focus. "What?" he snarled, then he saw Joe waving frantically and pointing toward the ranch. Spider looked and it took him a moment to wake up and realize that the ranch was now all dark. He could hardly contain his excitement and reached over and tugged at J.D.'s sleeve. "They're out now. J.D. They're out. They're out."

"I see. I see. I see. Dummy. O.K. guys, bring up Matilda. Come on Spider, and be quiet!"

The gang sprang into action upon J.D.'s order.

Spider mounted his bike and stood ready for J.D.'s signal. The other boys went into the bushes and brought up a rickshaw type home-made cart. It was a strange looking contraption, like a big box or shipping crate mounted upon bicycle wheels with two long rails in front, and with a six speed mountain bike between those rails to pull it. Ugly Joe pedalled as Wimp and Creep helped to push from behind, and as they negotiated between the trees in the dark, J.D., who was trying to direct them, stood a little bit too close and one wheel of the vehicle ran right over his tennis shoe. It hurt. In pain, J.D. grabbed his foot and, balancing on the other, hopped up and down. He wanted to scream out loud, but fearing discovery, stifled his voice, squeezing his lips tightly together, making instead a sound that was similar to air escaping from the pinched mouth of a party balloon.

"Fffffugggerrrappllllppptttt."

Spider couldn't help himself. J.D. just looked too danged funny hopping around on one foot like that, and he let out a giggle, which echoed throughout the forest. "Mfft Mfttt, hmmickle gick gickle gick." The minute he did that he knew he had made a big mistake, because it made J.D. even madder. J.D. hopped right over to where Spider sat on his bike, and jerking the tattered black leather cap off his head, swatted Spider across the face, back and forth four times. Whack! Whack! Whack! Whack!

"That will teach you to be quiet."

Having vented his frustration and anger, and relieving some of his pain in the process, J.D. turned to the gang, who all stood waiting patiently until he was finished roughing Spider up.

"Well," J.D. exclaimed, "What the heck are you guys waiting for? Let's go get that cow." With that, J.D. put his cap snugly back on his head, mounted his bike, and rode down the embankment and into the meadow toward the cows, with the gang all riding closely behind him like a bunch of wild, marauding Indians in a silent movie.

Bessie Cow looked up from her dinner of grass. Her ears raised, chewing her cud, she contemplated the five weird animals on wheels riding straight for her, then realizing the impending danger, bolted suddenly away, pulling away from her suckling calf as she darted off.

J.D. swung a lariat high above his head in a big circle as he came nearer to the dumbfounded calf, frozen in her tracks. Swish, swish, swish it went as it cut through the dew-laden night air. But before J.D could get close enough to drop the noose over the calf's neck, she bolted and bounded away.

Hidden in the deep grass was a rut that J.D. could not possibly have seen, but his front bike tire found it with no trouble at all. Before J.D. knew it, his bike was jolted to a sudden stop, the rear wheel came off the ground as the front buried itself in the turf, and he was thrown over the handlebars and flying through the air like a shot duck crashing to earth. He crashed to the ground, tumbled over once, then began sliding on his belly in the wet greenery.

Meanwhile, Spider tried to corner the frightened animal as several of the other boys closed in. The loop of his lariat hissed through the air as he twirled it above his head. When he finally let it go, the rope hit the bounding baby high on the right side. It balanced there for just a split second, then slid off. Before Spider knew what was happening, his front tire went over the rope and started winding it up. The bike stopped, shuddered, then fell over. Spider kept rolling over and over, the rope winding all around him as he tumbled. By the time he stopped rolling he was completely wound up, like string on a kite stick, and the calf was racing away with the other boys still in hot pursuit.

J.D. was up and back on his bike, speeding after the critter before you could say Rumpelstiltskin. He wound his lasso up, then swung it into the air above him as he rode, increasing the speed of the twirl with each and every round. Whoooooshh! Whoooooshh! Whooooshh! Whoosh! Whoosh!

Riding straight down the pasture, he waited for the rest of his gang to turn the frightened animal in his direction, then with jaw clenched in a look of desperate determination, he closed in. Closer, closer, closer. And, when he was right beside the calf, he dropped the loop over its neck. It was a perfect catch, the loop falling clean over the head without even touching the ears, then J.D. jammed on his brakes, holding on tight to the rope and skidding to a stop. The lax rope skittered across the grass, then became taut as the little calf reached the very end of her run. J.D. braced himself. He planted both boots, heels down in the ground, holding tightly with both hands, then he felt the rope slip and burn his palms. He gripped tighter and the rope stopped as the calf was jerked clear off her feet by the weight of her own body. Then like a rodeo cowboy, J.D. ran along the taut line, and dived on the fallen animal as she struggled to get up. By this time Spider had regained his feet and he and all the other boys ran in, throwing themselves one by one upon the downed animal in one big dog pile. Quickly, J.D. put a rope tie on her legs, then stood up and waved for Ugly Joe to bring the cart in. It was done quickly and silently. The tailgate was dropped and the boys wrestled and pushed the little calf into the box. Then, locking the tailgate, and with Ugly Joe pedaling and the other boys pushing, they got the wagon across the meadow, up the slight embankment and out onto the little dirt road that bordered the meadow. Creep and Wimp followed behind, brushing all the cart tracks away with a tree branch, then J.D. and the other boys mounted their bikes and they all rode away into the darkness. As they disappeared down the dirt road, the stillness of the night air was broken by the plaintive "Moooooooo" of the mother cow, searching in vain for her kidnapped baby.

CHAPTER FIVE

Devlin's Crossing was not far from Miners Oaks but it was a town totally different in character, and as the local folks all liked to say, going from one town to the other was like going to another planet. The towns were definitely different worlds. That had been a deliberate act of their common founders, who had a desire to keep heaven separated from hell in a very real sense.

Miners Oaks had been a rich town because of the Silver found there back in 1880, and those first wealthy and educated citizens wanted it to remain a clean and beautiful place to live and raise their families. So, Devlin's Crossing, not far away, was where all the outlaws went to entertain themselves; a rough and ready place where drinking and gambling and womanizing went on twenty four hours a day, seven days a week; a town where they put all the ugly factories, the feed lots and the slaughterhouse; the railroad yard and station, and everything else that nobody wanted to see, or even admit existed. It was where the miners and the cowboys of bygone years had lived. There were many stories told about gun fights and murders in Devlin's Crossing. But when the silver disappeared, most of the population slowly drifted away, disappearing into oblivion like wisps of dandelion fuzz on a warm autumn breeze.

There was a new two lane highway through town now, and a truck stop, but the character of the place hadn't changed at all. It was still a town where it was not safe to walk on the streets at night, and no respectable citizen would want to be seen there in the light of day, unless it was on business or absolutely necessary. It was a town that had a very ominous look and feeling. Even the air had the dank and smoldering odor of danger about it, like the smell of dying and decay.

J.D. and the boys rode quietly past the graffiti-marked buildings, trash can lined alleys, down the litter filled gutters of the back streets in the worst part of Devlin's Crossing. Carefully avoiding being seen, they passed only a few stray cats rummaging for food in the garbage cans, a few stray dogs prowling in a pack, and the inevitable sleeping drunk in a filth littered doorway.

J.D. rode way ahead, like an Indian scout, peering up and down the streets, making certain that no one was about, then signaled to the gang when it was safe to come along with the cart. Ugly Joe pedalled the bike pulling the cart while Wimp, Creep and Spider brought up the rear.

Through the darkened streets, past barred windows with broken glass they went into the depths of the narrow streets of the old industrial area until they came to a very narrow cobble-stone paved, dead-end alley. There, they turned and entered, with Spider remaining at the mouth of the alley as a lookout. Spider parked his bike against the crumbling brick wall, then, looking around, pulled a spray can out of his jacket and began to spray "SKUNKS" on the brick face of the building. J.D.'s head snapped around when he heard the hiss of the spray can. He dropped his bike and marched angrily over, stepping up behind Spider, grabbed his hand and wrenched the spray can away from him.

"What do you think you're doing, you idiot?" he snapped. "You leaving the cops a love note telling them that the Dirty Skunks were conducting a little illegal business here?" J.D. angrily threw the can away over a nearby fence. It made a clatter as it hit and rolled. A startled cat let out a scream and darted away into the night.

"Aw, gee J.D., I wasn't thinking of that."

"No kidding. You wasn't thinking at all, dummy. To think you have to have a brain, and you don't have one. Now you stay here and keep your stupid eyes open. And, don't do nothing else unless I say so. Got it?"

"Sure, J.D. I got it."

The gang was backing the cart up to the loading dock at the end of the alley as J.D. arrived, and climbed the three rotten wooden steps to the dock, above which was a single light in a huge green reflector dish. From the tin overhanging roof above was an old sign with peeling paint that read, MANNING'S MEAT MARKET, and under that in barely legible Old English print it said, "Fresh from the farm."

There was a large metal sliding door for loading freight in and out of the building, but it had a smaller regular sized door in it on the left side so that people could go in and out without opening the larger door. Beside this door there was a doorbell with a sign under it saying, "Ring for service." J.D. pushed the button and from somewhere inside the building you could hear the hollow sound of the bell clanging away. There was a quiet time while the boys all waited, listening. Then came the sound of footsteps, growing closer. They heard the sound of the bolt being withdrawn and the creaking of the rusty old hinges as the door was pulled slightly ajar. Through the small slice of opening J.D. peeked to see the rotund figure of a man in a blood spattered white apron and hat, who held a large meat axe in front of him as though for protection.

"It's me, Manning--J.D."

Manning peered out to see if there was anyone else around in the alley, then pulled the door open just far enough for J.D. to slip inside, then slammed it behind them. "Anybody see you come through town?"

"Not a soul."

"O.K. Help me with the big door. Let's make it quick."

J.D. helped Manning push the big door back, then waved at his boys to unlock the tailgate of the wagon. Quickly, they pulled and pushed the little calf across the dock and into the meat market, then the big door was quickly slid back into place leaving just Manning, J.D. and the calf inside. Together they pushed her onto a scale and J.D. held her steady as Manning adjusted the counterbalancing weights on the scale.

Manning's huge bushy eyebrows hid the sly way that he shot a glance at J.D. and his heavy and friendly voice disguised his clever slight of hand as he directed J.D.'s attention away from his manipulation of the scale. "Hold her steady," he said. "No, don't lean on her. You trying to get more weight on that scale to cheat me?"

"Naw, Manning. I wouldn't do that."

Manning's heavy finger on the back side of the scale arm, where J.D. could not see it, made the cow read a lot lighter than she really was. "O.K., that's 201 pounds at fifty cents a pound." Manning reached under his stained apron and into his pants pocket and withdrew a large roll of bills. "That's seventy eight dollars." He hoped that J.D. wasn't too good at math as he started counting the bills into the kid's open palm. "Sixty, seventy, seventy-five, seventy-eight."

Manning tied the calf to a post as J.D. fumbled through the bills. "You'd better go now. It wouldn't be good for you or the guys to be seen here. You know what I mean?" He went to the door and pulled the bolt back.

"Hey, wait a minute, Manning. "There's only seventy one bucks here," J.D. complained.

"Oh really?...Gee... Imagine that... I guess I thought that one of those fives was a ten. Ho, ho, ho, ho. The light is not too good in here, and my eyes, well, you know." He reached for his roll and slapped another five and two ones in J.D.'s hand.

"That's more like it."

"You'd better get going now, before someone sees you."

"Right."

Manning skillfully guided J.D. out the door, waved to the other boys, then quickly closed it behind him.

"Come on guys," J.D. said waving the cash so they could all see it.

"How much did your stepdad give you? Spider asked.

"I told you never to call him that," J.D. snapped.

"How come?" Spider asked, meekly.

"Because that word makes him mad, and it makes me mad too, and that's all you need to know. You got it?"

"Okay, J.D., I got it. So, how much did we get this time?"

"Only fifty bucks. It was a small calf."

"It didn't look that light," Wimp commented.

"You callin' me a liar?" J.D. retorted angrily.

"Anybody calls me a liar better be ready to fight."

"I didn't mean it. It was only a joke," Wimp said, cowering before J.D."

"Okay then," J.D. said, "Let's make it over to the hideout. We'll split the loot there." Then he got on his bike and took off with all the gang following behind.

On the table in the meat market was a very large and shiny knife. Manning picked it up and went to the grinding wheel where he began to sharpen. The sound of the wheel and the shrill sound that the knife made upon it caused the calf to perk up her ears and look in his direction. What she didn't know was that within a matter of hours she would be nothing more than 250 pounds of packaged meat in Mr. Mannings glass display case.

CHAPTER SIX

The sunrise was spectacular over Miners Oaks on Wednesday morning. Roosters crowed from nearby farms, and the smell of eggs and bacon hovered in the air outside Millie's cafe on Main Street. A dog barked at the postman as he walked by on his way to work, and birds were singing from the trees that now had golden leaves. Soon there were a few cars on the single main street, and people walking about doing their daily chores. The dew evaporated from the grass by ten, and it began to warm up. By noon it was seventy eight degrees. A perfect day.

The little red light on the new telephone answering machine was blinking when Sheriff George Smith came back from lunch about one o'clock, but because he hardly ever remembered to check it, he just hung his jacket up, put the coffee pot on, sat at his desk and opened a copy of "Field and Stream" Magazine and began reading without even noticing it.

Deputy Jim opened the door and came in with a cheery "Good afternoon, Sheriff." He was young and very good looking but skinny to the point of appearing emaciated so that his uniform fit loosely.

"Afternoon," the Sheriff said putting his magazine aside. "Well, you're right on time for your first day on the job. That's good. I like a man who is punctual."

"Well, that's one thing I am good at. Being on time. But I'm not used to coming to work in the afternoon. That might take some getting used to."

"Right. Well, I can understand that. I'm strictly a day person myself. I like to be home with the little woman when the sun goes down. But I've been putting in twelve hour days for a long time 'cause there's things to do early, and things to do late. I'm glad you're here. This way you can take some of the load off me. I'll be here in the morning, then you come in after lunch and stay a bit later in the evening."

"Fine. Fine. Sounds real good to me, Sheriff."

"So, you can sleep in a bit in the mornings if you want to." There was a loud squeek as the Sheriff leaned back in his old oak swivel desk chair. So far back that it seemed as if he might fall right over. Jim made a move to catch him, but then noticed that he didn't need to.

"I've got to put some oil on that," the Sheriff said. "Been so busy here that I've had to let lots of little things like that go. Now that you're here, Jim, maybe I can make a list and we can get caught up on some of this stuff."

"Right. Well sure. I can. I mean I will; I'm usually up with the sun. I like to run in the mornings. You know, kind of keep in shape just in case I ever have to chase anyone, or something. But I surely can adapt. I'm very adaptable. I was here early, walking around and kind-of familiarizing myself with the layout of the town. Just killing time until it was time to come to work, you know."

"Very good. That could come in handy in an emergency. It's bad when you got someplace to go in a hurry, and you don't know your way around. Course, we haven't had an emergency in a coon's age here in Miners Oaks, but you just never know about stuff like that. There could be one some of these days."

"Yep. That's so. Say, that's quite a police car you have parked out front, er, maybe I should say police wagon. I couldn't help noticing that it looks brand new, even though it's aged a bit."

"1937 Ford Woody station wagon," the Sheriff said proudly. "I always said that we would get a new police car when it broke down, but it never did. It's a classic now, I guess. They only built a few thousand of them--110 horse-power V/8 engine with a three speed manual transmission. She runs over these country roads like a jackrabbit. Not that I drive her fast, except when we go to Flagstaff. Oh, I opened her up a couple of times. Ooooew! She will run. Had her over 90 once. Me and that old car have kind of become good friends over the years, and she's never let me down. Summer, winter, you name it, she never failed to start and run. I had her completely re-built and painted last year and she is a beautiful lady now and everybody for miles around knows when they see her coming that it's Sheriff George Smith from Miners Oaks. I don't guess any other police department in America has a vehicle that brings so much class to the job."

"She's a real beauty alright," Deputy Jim agreed. "Say, Sheriff," he added, scratching his head, "is that a white hair I see there on your collar?"

George reached for his shirt collar and pulled a handful of white fur from it.

"Oh," he said, "it's our new baby, Snowball."

"Snowball?"

"It all happened yesterday. When I first woke up.

You see, it was like this: At first I thought I heard the wind making a slight sigh as it passed my bedroom window, it does that sometimes. But, as I came up from my dreams and listened more closely, I could tell that it was a tiny "meeeoow" from outside somewhere. Must be from next door, I thought, because Tigger, our twelve year old big orange cat, patrols our yard like a warrior Hun. It's his territory and any cat that dares to enter it is doomed to deadly combat. Yep, ol' Tigger has thoroughly trounced quite a few cats that tried, and chased even the biggest and bravest transgressors away with their fur a-flyin'. He's quite a cat. Well, anyway, I sort of ignored that sound, not hearing it no more, then, after one bowl of oatmeal with sliced peaches on top, two eggs and two cups of coffee, and a stack of buckwheats, I turned the radio off and opened the back door on my way out to the garage. But as I turned to lock the back door, my eye caught something bright and shiny, sparkling kind of in the sun. I turned and saw this tiny pure white kitten with sky blue eyes just a sitting there by the rocks bordering my wife's rose bushes, staring at me. Then the little guy let out a real loud "meeooow" and walked toward me, then I saw Tigger. He was just sitting quietly nearby, sunning himself, making no move to attack the little critter. I was amazed. He was accepting this little cat in his yard and making no fuss at all. That was a first for him. The little cat looked up at me and went "Meeeeeoooow! again, so danged loud and you could almost hear him saying "Daddy" in that cry, so, with one hand I scooped the little guy up. It was a her. A little dirty but otherwise lookin' fine and healthy, and she started to purr just the second I touched her. I held her up and looked her over."

My wife, Christine, who was just behind me--she always follows me out the door to kiss me goodbye in the morning--looked and smiled and I said to her, "I wonder whose cat this is?"

"Well," Christine said, hearing that loud purr coming from this tiny white ball of fur, "It surely appears to be your cat now."

"She looks a little skinny," I said. Then I went back into the kitchen and put a bowl of food down for her. Tigger came walking in, strutting his stuff to show us all what a tough guy he was, and still king of the territory, but he just looked at this little cat as it ate up its dish of food, took a quick sniff of her, then strutted on into the living room to find himself a comfortable place to take another nap. "I guess that means he approves of our new cat," I said to Christine.

"Your new cat."

Christine was being very non-committal about the little kitten but I noticed a shiny kind-of glint in her eyes and the corners of her mouth turned up in a tiny smile each time the kitten did something really cute, and when she got the camera out and started taking pictures--well, I knew that it was all over. Ain't it funny how you can read someone's thoughts when you been married for forty years, even though they don't say nothin'."

"Well, I've never been married," Jim said. "Not that I ain't had my chances. But I surely know what you mean."

"We'll have to get her fixed," Christine told me. "Two cats is enough for any house."

"I think I'll call her snowball," I told her, and she agreed that it would be a good name for an all-white fluffy baby cat. Anyway, that's how we got our new pet, and that's where the white hair comes from."

"I like cats too," Deputy Jim said. "By the way Sheriff, what is that blinking red light there on your desk?"

"Oh gosh," the Sheriff said sitting up in that old oak chair. "Squuueeeeeek!" it went. "Remind me to oil that spring today, will you? That's my new telephone answering machine. We just got that thing in the other day and I'm not used to it yet...my gosh," Sheriff George said in surprise. "It's a message. I wonder how long it's been on there."

"Ever since I came in, at least," Jim said. "It's been a blinkin' since then."

"I'd better see who it is." The Sheriff pushed the play button and the machine rewound then started to play the message.

"George, dad blast it," a voice said. "I ain't used to these gol-danged machines. New fangled stuff." Then a girl's voice could be heard in the background saying, "Leave a message, Grandpa. Leave a message."

"O.K. Ginger. Er, this is Cooper, George. Could you give me a ring as soon as you get in? It's kinda important. Thanks." Click. Buzzzzz.

George picked up his old black dial type phone and dialed Cooper's number and let it ring a long time. "Hmmmm, no answer. He must be out feeding the chickens or something. Come on Deputy. Let's take a ride out there. And remind me later to oil that dad-gummed chair, will ya?"

Ten minutes later the Ford Woody rolled up the driveway to the Cooper farm and stopped by the front porch. George turned off the key but the engine just kept on idling. Then it missed a couple of times, coughed once, then, emitting a loud BANG!, stopped, blowing a huge cloud of black smoke out the tailpipe.

"Cheap gas," George said. "They don't make nothin' like they used to."

"You sure it's the gas?"

"Yep. I'll get a quart of pure alcohol from the paint

store on the way back and put it in the gas tank and she will run like a champion from then on. You'll see."

"That right?" Jim commented. "Gee, I wish I could do that with my car, but these newer ones have fuel injection and the system has a lot of rubber o-rings in it that alcohol will rot out."

"That so?" the Sheriff said opening his door. "Well, so much for modern technology. Seems like it's two steps back for every one taken forward, sometimes. Come on, Jim. Let's go see what ol' Mr. Cooper wants."

A big red-haired dog was napping in the overstuffed chair on the front porch. He opened his eyes at the sound of the car, and watched with sleepy interest as the doors opened and the occupants alighted and started toward the house.

Jim was just ahead of the Sheriff and his cowboy boots hit the wooden steps first. The dog leaped from the chair, jumping at Jim. Up on his hind legs, his front paws on Jim's shoulders, he was almost as tall as the deputy. Jim grabbed the dog's collar with one hand, his pistol with the other, drew it, and cocked the hammer. Sheriff George grabbed his wrist. "It's okay, Jim, he said. He's just a big puppy. "Jeez," Jim said, breathing heavily, I thought he was going for my throat."

"He wouldn't hurt a fly," a melodic voice came from behind the screen door. Behind it Jim could see the figure of Ginger Cooper in shadow. It was a nice figure, even in that light.

"Errk!" Jim said, pushing the licking dog away, "He has . . . doggie breath!"

"Grandpa," Ginger called out, "we have company."

"Who is it?" a voice came from within. The Sheriff moved to the screen. "It's me, Mr. Cooper. Sheriff George. And, I brought my new Deputy out to meet you. Jim Cranberry."

"Well, what happened to Rick?" Ginger asked. She seemed surprised that he had been replaced.

"Oh, he got a higher paying job over in Phoenix. Managing a Burger King, or something like that. I think he had a girl over that way too." Ginger bit her lip. "Oh," she said. "Well, he was kind of stuck up anyway. Hi, Jim. I'm Ginger."

Jim was still trying to ward off the insistent kisses of the big dog and hold on to his hat at the same time. "Hi," he said. "Pleased to meet you, Miss Ginger."

"Get hold of that dog," Grandpa Cooper said, opening the screen door so that they could both come out, "before she licks that poor fella to death. Well, hi there, George. I sure am glad to see you. Left a message on that dad blasted new fangled machine of yours."

"We got it. That's why we're here."

"Sorry to bring you way out here on such a small matter, but to me it's a really big thing. Hey, who is this?"

"This here is Jim. He's my new Deputy."

"Good to meet you," Cooper said extending his big rough hand and squeezing Jim's with a powerful shake. "How come I ain't seen you hereabouts? I thought I knew just about everybody."

"Oh, I'm from over Kingman way," Jim said, trying to get loose from the powerful grasp of the old farmer, ward off the dog, and hold onto his hat all at the same time.

"No kidding. Used to have a cousin that lived over there. He was workin' in a steel mill, but the place blew up, and they never even found a piece of him. How come you're over here, Jim?"

"Well, cause I got this job, as Deputy."

"Oh, sure. I see. Well, as I said, I'm sorry to bring you both out here on such a small matter. But I got three calves missing."

"Missing cows. That could be rustlers. That's no small matter, Mr. Cooper. We gotta stop that wherever it starts, before it gets out of hand."

"Er, could I have my hand loose?" Jim said timidly.

"Oh, sorry." Cooper said, letting it go. "I forgot I had it." The big dog ran to the chair on the porch and got a big red rubber ball, then, ran right back and started jumping up on Jim again, licking and slobbering all over him.

"She really likes you," Ginger commented. "And she just loves to chase that ball."

"Oh, she does, huh?" Jim wrestled the ball out of the big dog's mouth and threw it as far as he could, then happily watched as she ran off after it.

"Well, to me it's a really big deal, if you catch my drift," Cooper said, stepping down off the porch and walking out toward the pasture. The Sheriff, Jim, and Ginger followed as he continued. "I'm just a small time farmer, and it's all I can manage just to try and feed the two of us, so when I start losing cows, that's real serious."

"Yes, it's a terrible thing when a man is robbed. I know that feeling," the Sheriff said sympathetically. "It gets you right in the pit of your stomach. And you say that they took three of your calves last night?"

"Well no. They got ONE last night, ONE the week before, and ONE the week before that. That makes three altogether."

"You mean this has been goin' on for three weeks and you didn't tell anyone? Why the heck didn't you call us before now?"

"Well, dang it, George. I didn't know it myself. You see, at first I just thought I was counting wrong, or that one had wandered off and might come back. Cows do that, you know. So, we looked, but we couldn't find it. Then, I thought it might be a coyote got it. Then, when the second one turned up missing, I was pretty near sure it was a coyote. Or maybe even a mountain lion."

"I ain't seen a mountain lion hereabouts for a spell, but it's possible," the Sheriff said as they moved out toward the field.

With their backs turned toward Jim and Ginger they didn't notice the big red pooch bounding happily back with the ball in her mouth. Slobbering doggie spit all over Jim, she jumped up on him nearly knocking him over. Jim wrestled with the ball, jerking it out of the animal's mouth, then pretended to throw it, with a big sweep of his arm. Big Red ran off looking for the ball as Jim concealed it behind his back.

"So, I got my rifle out, cleaned it and oiled her up real good, and went a lookin' for the varmint. But my eyesight ain't what she used to be. Got three chickens, a hawk, and a rabbit. And someone's pet guinea pig. Gee, I felt bad about that, but how was I to know? He was hidin' in the bushes and his eyes glowed in the dark just like a big ol' mountain lion. Scared the tar outa' me, so I aimed right between those eyes and pulled the trigger. Ya' know, people shouldn't ought to let their pets run loose like that."

Big Red went like a streak of fire out into the field, around a cow twice, then back towards Jim, as the Sheriff and Cooper walked ahead talking.

"And just exactly when did you begin to suspect that it wasn't a coyote or a mountain lion, Mr. Cooper?

"Well, last night, while my granddaughter and me was seein' a movie over in Big Town. One of those horror movies it was. Gee, it was a real exciting picture show too."

Deputy Jim and Ginger moved up close to where Cooper and the Sheriff were standing in the middle of the meadow, and Ginger was looking Jim over with big calf-eyes, and she seemed to be glowing from within. She liked what she saw.

Big Red came running back and was circling the four of them at full speed and barking all the while, but they all had other things on their minds and they just ignored her. Jim's ears perked up when he heard about the movie they had just seen, and he asked what the name of it was.

"Oh, it was called, ahhh, it was called... What was that picture called, Ginger?"

"The Teenage Monsters of Halloween," Ginger replied without ever taking her eyes off of Jim.

"Yeah. That's it. The Teenage Monsters of Halloween. A real good one too. Scared the pants off'n me."

"Gosh, I guess I'll just have to see that one," Jim said. "I really love those horror films."

The Sheriff, noticing that the conversation was getting sidetracked, cleared his throat, then asked, "So, when you and Ginger got back from the movies, then that was when you noticed that you had three cows missing?

"Well no Sheriff, not exactly. You see, I counted them when we got home and there was eighteen. It was in the morning when I went out to feed the chickens that I noticed that there seemed to be less, so I counted them again and there was only seventeen."

Big Red was making such a fuss that she was disturbing the conversation, so Sheriff George turned to Jim and said, "You gonna throw that ball so's we can get on with this here investigation?"

"Oh, sure, Sheriff," Jim said. Then he wound up his arm like a major league pitcher and tossed the ball clear out of the meadow, over the trees, and onto the road beyond.

"Wow," Ginger said, "You got some arm there." Then she

moved in real close and started to feel Jim's arm. He tried to make a muscle for her.

"I used to play Little League," Jim said proudly. "I was pretty good too."

Cooper frowned. "I used to count them in the mornings, but since this started happening, I got to counting them in the morning and again at night," Cooper said. Then he noticed Ginger feeling Jim's Arm. "Ginger! What are you doin' out here? Go get lunch started. You fellas want to stay for lunch?"

Jim started to say yes, but then decided to defer to the Sheriff, so he just bit his tongue, and said nothing.

"No thanks Mr. Cooper," the Sheriff said. We have a pretty full schedule today, and I've got to show Jim here the ropes and get him broke in so's he can make the rounds for me later tonight. We'll make a full report on your missing cows. Anything else you can tell us?"

"Not that I can think of. You gotta help me on this, Sheriff. Pretty soon all of them will be gone if this keeps up. Then all I'll have is the bank payments, and no cows.

"We'll do what we can Mr. Cooper. Jim, you go take a look over there at the bank near the road and see if you can spot any tracks. It's a likely way out of this meadow and you just might find something."

"Sure thing, Sheriff."

Jim walked over and started examining the bank, pushing leaves aside with a branch from a tree, as Ginger headed back to the house, but on the walk she kept taking peeks over her shoulder at Jim. Looking at him made her feel good inside. She didn't exactly know why, but it did.

The sunlight glinted upon something shiny in the grass and the Sheriff stooped to pick it up."

"What's that you got there?" Cooper asked.

"Dunno. Piece of chrome plated metal off something. Look familiar to you?"

"Nope, can't say that it does."

Then Jim called out to them from the slope not far away.

"Sheriff. I found some tracks over here."

The Sheriff and Grandpa hiked quickly over to where Jim was waiting and took a good look at the ground where Jim pointed. Jim stooped down then and carefully wiped away the leaves and grass to uncover marks in the wet mud of the bank.

"See here," Jim said. "It's only part of a tire tread mark, but it's there. Looks like someone deliberately brushed these leaves and stuff over it to try and hide it. It's an old Indian trick."

The Sheriff stooped to take a closer look. "Sure does. Looks like a wheel barrow track, or motorcycle. Did you drive something up this bank, Mr. Cooper?"

"No sirree. Not me."

"I've got some plaster of Paris in a blue and white box in the back of the station wagon, Jim. Go get it. And, there's a little bucket there to mix it in too. Get a little water in that and we'll make a plaster cast of this track. We can send it over to the police lab in Flagstaff and see if they can identify it for us."

"Sure thing, Sheriff."

But before Jim could turn, there was a crashing noise from the nearby trees. All three men turned and looked up just in time to see Bernard Wheel fly down the path across the road, leap up a rise, fly through the air for about twenty feet, then disappear over a hill and out of sight into the forest.

Jim turned to the other two men, a look of surprise upon his face. "What the heck was that?"

Cooper and the Sheriff laughed and explained that it was only Bernard, a local boy who was known for his fancy bike riding. On the walk back to the station wagon to get the plaster, they told him all about him being an orphan, and about how Bernard got his bike, and how he was the fastest kid on wheels, and everything else they knew about Bernard.

"So nobody knows who he is or where he came from?" Jim asked.

"I tried everything that I knew how to do to try and find out," the Sheriff said, "but I had no luck. So, unless someone comes forward some day to tell us, we just may never find out."

"Seems really sad," Jim said as he mixed the plaster and poured it into the tire marks in the mud. "Really, really sad."

CHAPTER SEVEN

Beams of sunlight shone down through the tree tops, spreading out like blades of a fan, glowing in the rising mists, giving the forest a dream-like appearance. As Bernard guided Superbike along the narrow pathway through the giant redwood trees, a sudden mood came over him that he had never felt before. It was so peaceful. Everything was so perfect, and he felt so at home here; almost as if the forest was alive--like a mother, welcoming him into her open arms. He felt safe and warm, and happy.

Ahead was a path that Bernard had never seen before, and he wondered why. After all the times that he had explored the places around Lake Madera Azul, he thought that he had been on them all, but this one was new to him. He decided to take a look at it and see just where it went.

Riding down the leaf-littered trail, dodging through

trees, jumping over rocks, and roaring through ferns and shrubs, he couldn't help but notice the magical quality of the place, and although he'd been in this forest many times, this trail appeared as though no one had ever been here before. Maybe it had only been traveled by deer, bears, and other animals, he thought. Maybe he was even the very first human being to ever travel it. He didn't know that for sure, but it was neat to pretend that he was the first person to ever have been here. Anyway, he was the only person here now and that was the important part.

Then, as he rounded a bend in the trail, he smelled smoke and something cooking. He stopped and sniffed the air trying to see or smell where it was coming from. Then, peering through the trees far ahead, he saw a long thin plume of gray smoke that was wafting upwards through the leaves and branches and up into the light filtering down from the sky above. He rode nearer, following it by sight and smell until he saw that it was coming from a campfire in a clearing far below near a stream. Moving ever closer until he was very near, Bernard stopped his bike, alighted and moved to peer around a tree, through the ferns to peek unnoticed down into the clearing below.

There was a strange man there. About the same age as his teacher, Mr Brown, he thought. That would be about thirty-five. But this man was dressed in clothing unlike Bernard had ever seen. His coat was dark green with large shiny silver buttons and it was so long that it came nearly to his knees. Around his waist was a very wide and shiny black belt with a huge silver buckle, and he was wearing knee high black boots. And, as if this were not strange enough, he had a very big and colorful bird perched on his right shoulder. This bird had fluffy yellow feathers from head to tail, but with bright blue and red and green splashed all over it as though it had gone wild in a paint store. The sight of this bird almost made Bernard laugh, because they were bright and happy colors. They made him want to smile and grin, but he got control of these wild emotions that swept through him, because he did not want to be embarrassed by being discovered peeking at the stranger. He slid back behind the tree and sat for a time, until he got the laugh out of his system, then turned and peeked around the tree again. Bernard had never seen a bird like that, or a man like this. He watched with great curiosity as the man sat on a big fallen tree log, turning a fish on a stick over the campfire. The smell of the smoke and the fish wafted up through the trees and bushes to Bernard, going right up his nose. Curious, he moved even closer, being careful to be very quiet so that he would not be seen or heard. He was careful not to step on leaves that would make a crunching sound, or to touch branches that could make noise too. It was an old Indian trick that his friend Jojo had taught him.

Walking Superbike down the trail, Bernard circled the clearing, getting much closer so that he could get into position to get a better look at this very curious sight.

The colored bird on the man's shoulder suddenly turned, flapped his wings, and made a squawking sound, "Aaaaawwwk!" Then the man put his hand up to quiet the bird, and without turning, said in a voice loud enough for Bernard to hear, "That was some pretty incredible bike riding, son." It was a strong voice, which vibrated through the trees, making the leaves tremble, but it was nice and warm and friendly as well. Bernard liked the sound of it.

Looking quickly around to see if anyone else was there, Bernard scanned the forest, but saw no one. He wondered if this man was speaking to him. He must be. But how could he tell that he was there? Maybe he was just talking to that big colorful bird. No, birds don't ride bikes.

"You're welcome to come and join us for some fish if you like. There's plenty," the man said.

Bernard stuck his head around the tree. "You talking to me?" he said, without really knowing why. It was almost as if someone else had said the words for him.

"I'm talking to the red headed boy with the real pretty bike, hiding in the bushes behind me," the man said without turning. "Come on and pull up a tree, and join us."

Bernard wondered if it was all right, then decided it was. He pushed Superbike near the campfire, parked her against a tree, then turned and saw the man and the bird from the front for the first time. They both seemed to be smiling at him, the bird through that big yellow beak and the man, with perfect white teeth shining through a perfectly trimmed and shaped beard. Even his eyes held the look of friendship in their shimmering blue.

"Have a seat," the man said.

"Awwwwwk, hello. Tweet. Have a seat."

"How did you know that I was there?" Bernard asked. "Some things you just know. You sense them. Like a dog that just knows if you like him. Like homing pigeons that can find their way home from anyplace in the world, no matter where you take them. The way you know when someone is standing behind you, even if you can't see them. I guess that there is no way to really explain it. Some call it intuition, pre-cognition, extra-sensory perception, whatever words you like to use to try and explain it. It just happens. Everyone has that ability. Some don't know how to use it, but they can learn. That's how I knew that someone was standing behind me in the bushes. Come in, sit down. Join us. Have some of this fish. It's delicious."

Bernard's eyes darted quickly around the campsite. He saw a little tent made of silk-like green material nearby under a tree, and a bedroll near it. There was a fishing pole and some pots and pans, the man and the bird, and that was all.

"You live out here in the forest?"

"Yep. I guess you could say that. We do. Me and my feathered friend here. We have the big sky for our roof and all this beauty to call home. Isn't it the most perfect place to live that you have ever seen?"

"Well sure. I guess so. It's nice all right. But how come I've never seen you around here before?"

"Well, it's a very big world son, and it wouldn't exactly be unusual if you didn't meet one single person in this whole big universe. Trying to find me would be sort of like trying to find one particular grain of sand out there in the dunes. And, besides I move around a lot, going from place to place, never staying any place too long. I'm just passing through this little corner of the universe right now, and that's probably why you haven't seen me. But the weather is so good here, and I love this place, so I might just stay here a while this time. You'll probably see me around now. What do they call you, son?"

"You mean my name?"

"Right. You do have a name, don't you?"

"Well, sure. It's Bernard. Bernard. What's yours?"

"You can call me Hal. And this is Senor Birdy."

"Senor Birdy? Is he a Mexican Parrot? I've never seen so many colors on one bird before."

"Actually, he's from a tiny far away place that you probably never heard of, but he speaks both Spanish and English. Don't you Birdy?"

"Tweet. Si si Senor. Want some fish Bernard? Awwwk. Tweet."

"Wow. That was neat. But how did he know my name?"

"He heard you say it. And, he's a very smart bird. Aren't you Birdy?"

"Awk. Smart bird, tweet."

"Does he know what he's saying, or is he just mimicking us?"

"Now that is a very good question. Only Senor Birdy knows, and he's not telling. He likes a mystery, you see. It keeps the mind interested, and working. How about some of this fish now. It's rainbow trout."

"Well, sure. I guess so," Bernard said, moving to take a seat on the big log near Hal.

"Bernard. That's an unusual name. How did you happen to get a name like that?" Hal offered Bernard a piece of smoking hot fish impaled upon a long sharp stick.

"Be very careful of that. You could burn your tongue. It's very hot."

Bernard blew on the fish to cool it off before taking a bite.

"I kind-of picked the name out myself," he said, then between bites he told Hal that he had seen a movie once where a big fluffy brown and white dog with big soft eyes saved some freezing people that got lost in a snow storm, and how it was a Saint Bernard dog, and how he just liked the name so much that he took it for his very own.

"Awwwk! Bernard," Senor Birdy squawked.

"Interesting. And have you ever saved anyone from freezing in the snow?"

"Heck no, Hal. Gosh. It doesn't snow here. Least not enough to freeze anyone, but it would be nice to save people from any kind of danger they might be in. I mean, if they needed you to, and you could help."

"A boy with ideas and principles. An admirable

quality in one so young. I like that."

"I like that. Awwk! I like that."

"Shhhhhh." Hal waved a no-no hand at Birdy, then offered some more trout to Bernard who gobbled up the last bite as though he hadn't eaten in a week.

"Well. What about the last name?" Hal asked.

"Wheel?" Bernard said between bites. "Bernard Wheel."

"Wheel? That's kind of an unusual name. You pick that one out too?"

"Yep. I picked that one out too. Mmmmm, the fish is really good. It was on account of the way I like bikes."

"Awk! Bikes?"

"Is that so? I always thought that babies got named by their parents. How come you got to pick your own name?"

"Well, it's kind of a long story," Bernard said, then he told Hal all about how he was left on Mrs. Mueller's doorstep when he was a baby and how she ran the home for homeless kids, and how she let him pick out his own name when he was old enough and wanted to.

"One day she said, 'Oh golly, you are getting too big to just be called Little Guy. I guess we ought to pick out a proper name for you.' And then I said, 'Well, if I'm big enough to get a proper name, then I'm big enough to pick it out for myself.' And Mrs. Mueller said, 'You're right.' And so I picked Bernard because of the dog, and Wheel because of my bike, since I don't have any parents."

"Everyone has parents, Bernard."

"Well, I mean, I just don't know who mine are. Maybe I'll find out someday, but for now, I just live with Mrs. Mueller, and she's really neat, and she's really just like a mom."

"I'll bet she is. She sounds like a very nice lady."

"A really nice lady. Aaawk!"

"I see you are wearing some knee pads. What are those for?"

"Oh, that's for soccer practice. The Blue Angels. We're having a game and we practice every night at my school. We're playing for the whole entire championship of the State of Arizona this coming Sunday."

"Really? Tell me about that. That sounds real interesting."

"Aaaawk. Tell me. Tell me."

"Okay," Bernard said, and started to tell Hal and Senor Birdy his story. He was having a good time and felt like he was already old friends with Hal and Senor Birdy.

Riding through the forest, not far away, were J.D., Spider, and the rest of the Dirty Skunk Gang. Ugly Joe cruised on ahead, speeding down a long hill. Then he made a wide sweep out through some trees, showing off for the other guys. It was then that he noticed the smoke rising in one straight plume above the trees down another little path. He rode out there to see what he could see, and parking his bike and climbing some small outcropping of rock where he could see down in the valley, he peered over.

He waved to the other boys, then put his finger up to his lips signaling for them to be quiet as they pulled up. The boys all dropped their bikes on the trail and climbed the rocks to where Joe waited. One by one they crawled to the edge and looked over.

"It's ol' goody goody two shoes," Spider quipped. "Bernard smarty pants Wheel."

"Where?" said J.D.

"Way down there in the clearing. At that campfire. See?" Spider pointed and J.D. sighted along his finger.

"Aha! I see him. He's eating something with some

hobo. I hope he eats a lot. I hope he stuffs himself real good."

"Why?" Spider asked, screwing his face into a horrible grimace.

"Don't do that," J.D. said, taking his hat and smacking Spider on the nose.

"Why boss? I'm just makin' a face."

"Yeah, well your face isn't funny. It's ugly and it makes me want to puke, so stop it."

"Okay. Okay. So why do you want Bernard to eat a big meal?"

"Because, stupid. With a full belly, maybe he won't be able to ride so fast. We'll just wait here until he leaves, then we'll run him down and teach that jerk something that he won't forget for a long long time."

Ugly Joe unwrapped a candy bar, threw the wrapper into the bushes, took a bite of it, and then asked through chocolate covered teeth, "How come you hate Bernard so much, J.D.?"

"That's my business," J.D. snapped as he jerked the candybar away from Ugly Joe and devoured it in one gigantic gulp.

Spider hesitated, then asked, "Well, I thought we was going over to the Seven-Eleven store to play video games? Who wants to sit out here in the forest and watch Bernard eat? He could be there for hours."

Joe chimed in then, "Yeah," he complained. "Let's go to the Seven-Eleven. We can steal some candy bars and play video games."

"I'm staying right here until Bernard leaves," J.D. said, folding his arms and leaning back against the big rock. Then his face took on a look of surprise and he yelled out.

"Ow."

He jumped up and Spider started wiping at his

back with his hands.

"You sat in a nest of red ants," Spider said.

"Eooooow! Get them off me."

Ugly Joe and Wimp helped brush the ants off, then when J.D. had calmed down a bit, Spider started to sweet talk him into leaving.

"Come on J.D., it's going to be dark soon. Let's go to the Seven-Eleven. That sissy Bernard will probably go right by there on his way home and we'll get him then."

"Okay, okay. Let's get out of here." So saying, they all crawled down the rock to their bikes and, with J.D. in the lead, they all rode on down the trail and out of the forest toward Miners Oaks.

Hal glanced briefly up toward the rocks at the top of the canyon as Bernard told him all about Mrs. Mueller and the kids that lived there with him.

"Little Mary is the smallest," Bernard said, "and she has this bad foot. She was born with it and she has to wear a special shoe so that she doesn't walk funny. Mrs. Mueller is trying to get enough money to have it operated on. She takes in laundry and she is even going to have a drink stand at the soccer game to try to get enough money to pay for the operation."

"Can't she get some help from the government for that?"

"Mrs. Mueller says that she wants the best doctor to do it, and the government won't pay for that, and besides, the government humiliates you when you ask for help, Mrs. Mueller says. They make you wait in lines and fill out all sorts of papers, and then you don't get the best hospital or the best doctor."

"I see."

"And some of the people in town will help too.

Anyway, she has time because the doctors say that Mary shouldn't do this operation until she is seven years old."

"Oh? Why is that?"

"I dunno. Something to do with the foot growing to a certain size before they will do it."

"Que sada muy grande noche suldano. Awwwkk!"

"What did he say?" Bernard asked. Senor Birdy had surprised him with the sudden burst of language.

"Nothing important. He just likes to jabber on sometimes." Hal put his plate aside and rubbed his stomach. "Now, that's what I call a good meal. You want some more, Bernard?"

"No thanks. Mrs. Mueller will have supper ready when I get home, and she'll be mad if I don't eat, so I have to leave some space."

"Then, I'll just finish this last bite myself. Mmmmm. Excellent. Well, this has been a great day. One of the best I can remember. A good fire, a good meal, and good friends to share it with. You just can't do better than that. You know, that sure is a neat bike you have there. I don't believe that I have ever seen one quite like it."

"That's because I built it myself," Bernard said proudly. "I call her Superbike."

"Really"

"Awwk! Superbike. Neat bike. Tweet, tweet!"

"Well, what I mean is, Mrs Mueller got me the frame, and Mr. Brown, my teacher at school, got the wheels at the church bazaar one Sunday, and then they put this bike together for me at Christmas. Then I got the idea to look for more parts from all the bikes that were being thrown out, and I looked for them on trash days. Then I collected all those parts and I kind of put them all together and made my own special kind of bike. It took me a long time to get it the way it is now. Isn't she awesome?"

"Well, she sure is a pretty bike, all right. You should be really proud of yourself."

"And she rides real good too. I'm always working on her, making improvements, and the more I do, the more I learn, and the more I learn, the better she gets. Mr. Duffy, he's the man who owns the gas station in Miners Oaks, he gave me some parts too, and let me use his grinder and work bench, and he showed me how to use a drill and stuff. Anyway, I tinkered with her until I got her to be just about the fastest bike in the whole world. At least the fastest in Miners Oaks. And I can jump real far too."

"Really? How far can you jump."

"Well, I never measured it exactly, but I practice every day on my way to school, and on the way home too, and I keep jumping farther and farther. And sometimes, when I feel exactly right, it feels like I can stay up there forever--just like flying through the sky. But then the wheel hits the ground, and I know that I can't really fly."

"Why not?"

"Well, cause, it's impossible. You can't really fly on a bike."

"Maybe. Then again, maybe you can. Not long ago people didn't believe you could fly at all. They thought all kinds of silly things until the Wright Brothers came along and flew. People used to believe that the world was flat, and that if you sailed to the end of it, you would fall off, and that the whole universe revolved around the earth, and that you couldn't talk to people in other countries, or send your picture around the world. But now you have airplanes, and telephones, and TV, and some men from Earth have even gone into space. Once they thought that all of these things were impossible. So, you see, nothing is really impossible. It's all just mind over matter. Anything is possible if you just believe that it is. Why, this whole universe is just a big ball of energy, and matter becomes energy, and energy becomes matter. They transform. Your scientist, Albert Einstein, had it almost right, E=MC squared. So, if you can generate sufficient belief, you can use that energy to transform and overcome any obstacle. Are you following this, Bernard?"

"Well, kind of. I mean, I read about Albert Einstein and his mathematical work, and my teacher, Mr. Brown tells us about some of this stuff."

"Right. Albert was on the right track, but he didn't follow it all the way to it's logical conclusions."

"Awwwwwwwk! Albert was cool."

"You mean that if I believe it enough, I can think myself into a longer jump on my bike?"

"Absolutely. Maybe, and I say maybe, you could even make Superbike fly. If you really and truly believe that you can."

"Wow, wouldn't that be neat--flying through the air like a bird on Superbike. Zooooomm. Gosh. It would be so much fun. But it's impossible."

"Aaaaaak. Mucho tarde. Tweet, tweet."

Hal suddenly stood up and looked up through the trees at the sky. He stood there for a long moment, closed his eyes, then opened them again. "It's getting dark, son. You'd better be getting home."

"Gee, you're right. I forgot all about the time and Mrs. Mueller will be wondering where I've been."

"It's been really nice talking with you, Bernard. It was fun."

"Me too. I mean, it was really nice meeting you, and Senor Birdy too."

Senor Birdy ruffled up his feathers and flapped his wings. "Aaawk! Bernard. Tweet. Bye Bye."

"I enjoyed our visit too," Hal said. "You are a very

interesting fellow, but you'd better go right home now, and be very careful tonight."

"Huh?"

"It can be dangerous riding through the forest at dusk. You think you can see all right, but in the failing light, your eyes can deceive you. You should take extra care when you can't see the dangers that might be lying just ahead of you."

"But it's not even dark yet."

"It will be soon. Just promise me that you will be careful, will you?"

"Well, okay, sure. Well, thanks for the fish and everything. Nice meeting you, Hal"

"And remember what I told you about mind over matter." Hal stood and picked up a small round stone, and began tossing it up and catching it. "Remember, with enough concentration you could probably make that bike of yours actually fly."

"Right. Well, goodbye. Er, will I see you again, Hal? I mean, are you going to stay here for a while?"

"Yes. We'll be here. For a time anyway. Stop by anytime."

"Aaawwwk! Stop by anytime, Bernard. Tweet."

"Oh, good. I mean, I'll be seeing you, Hal. See you, Birdy." Bernard mounted Superbike, then kicked off and started up the trail and out of the canyon, calling back as he rode off. "I'll see you around."

"Hasta la vista, Bernard. Aaawk!" Birdy called after him.

Hal was tossing the rock up, catching it, then tossing it up again and as Bernard disappeared into the trees, he tossed it into the air one last time, looked at it hard with one of his sky blue eyes, and the rock slowed, spun one more time, then stopped dead still as if frozen in time. Hal reached up and scratched his head for a long moment, keeping his eye firmly on the rock, then when he had finished scratching he reached out and closed his fist around it.

"He's a really nice boy," Birdy chirped.

"Yes," Hal replied. "I am very proud of him." So saying, he sliped the rock into his coat pocket, then turned and went back to the campfire.

The room where Mrs. Mueller did her cooking was the very picture of the perfect farm house kitchen. The kind you see on calendars and in magazines. An old wood stove, with all the copper pots hanging above it stood in one corner. The solid oak sideboard went all along one wall under the window with gingerbread curtains framing the view to the back with the mountains beyond. There was a big oak chopping block in the very middle of the room, and everything from top to bottom was as spotlessly clean and as perfect as any kitchen could be, and the smell of the room was flavored with the hundreds of spices and condiments that had been used here for years and years. This was confirmed by their prominent presence on the big shelf that went high along one wall, filled with all the tiny bottles of flavorings from all over the world. There was ginger, and sage, and cinnamon, nutmeg, and cardamon, and clove, and rosemary, and thyme, and paprika, cumin, basil, curry powder from India, and even bay leaves that Mrs. Mueller had grown in her very own garden in back of the house.

Now the smell of the roast intended for tonight's dinner filled the room, and Mrs. Mueller was just removing it from the oven, balancing the heavy pan on her pad as she carried it to the chopping block for cutting, as Bernard came dashing in through the back door all out of breath.

"Oh, there you are darling. I was getting worried. Where in the world were you?"

"Hi, Mrs. Mueller," Bernard said, going directly to her and planting a big kiss on her cheek. "I met this really nice man in the forest, his name is Hal, on my way home from soccer practice, and he has this big bird from South America, or someplace, that has a million colors in his feathers all over his body, and he talks, and his name is Senor Birdy. And he knew my name and he could say it. You should have heard him. He even speaks Spanish. Oh, he speaks English too, but he speaks Spanish too. It was so neat."

Bernard grabbed a hot pad and helped Mrs. Mueller with the pan until it was safely sizzling on the chopping block.

"Thank you Bernard," she said patting him on top of his carrot colored head. "But darling, you know that you have been told that it's not wise to talk to strangers. Especially strange men living in the forest with strange animals for friends. And don't forget that you made me a promise that you'd try to be on time from now on. You know how I feel about being punctual, and keeping promises."

"Yes ma'am, I know. I'm sorry."

"It's something that you need to work on, young man. You are just too much of a dreamer."

"I'm sorry. I just was having such a good time, I forgot how late it was. Actually, it was Hal and Senor Birdy that told me it was time to go home, because I was having such a good time that I just forgot, and it was getting dark and all. Do you think I could learn to speak Spanish, Mrs. Mueller?"

"Of course you can, Bernard. You have to take some kind of language in high school to qualify for going to college, so if you want to, you could take Spanish. But, just who is this mysterious stranger living out in the forest, anyway?"

"Well, ummm. I don't know. I guess he was just camping or fishing or something, and he had a tent. He says he travels around a lot. Anyway, his name is Hal, and he's a really nice man. He was fun to talk to, and he told me lots of interesting stuff."

"You must be careful about people that you don't know, Bernard. I wouldn't want anything to happen to my precious little boy."

"Aw, I know, Mrs. Mueller. Even Hal told me to be careful after dark. But I'm home now, and I'm okay, see? I'm safe, see? Nothing to worry about at all."

"Well, all right. Now you go and wash your hands and face real good and get ready for supper. We have to eat a bit early tonight because I want you to go out with little Mary while she sells her Girl Scout cookies, and help her."

"But don't you need me to help you here, with the dishes?"

"Yes, I do, but Mary insists on doing her part selling those cookies, and she is much too little to be out on the streets alone in the evening, so, I want you to go with her."

"Awww."

"No complaining. Remember she helped you polish your bike last Saturday."

"But she didn't do it right. She thought the grease was bike wax and she smeared it all over my bike, and I had to clean it all off."

"That doesn't matter. She thought she was helping, and it's a person's intentions that are the important thing."

"Right. Okay."

"Now go get the hands washed, young man."

"All right."

Mrs. Mueller watched him as he disappeared onto the back porch where the sink and soap was, then she took her hot mitten off and went to the old oak crank phone and turned the handle three times hard." Sheriff? George, this is Emma. Sorry to bother you at home, but I wanted to ask a little favor. No, no, nothing urgent, I just wanted you to look into something for me. A stranger--maybe just a fisherman--in the forest..."

CHAPTER EIGHT

Little Mary ran out the front door. The sound of her feet making different noises as the soft shoe hit, then the big leather one with the extra soles and metal plate in it clumped across the big wooden porch. Down the steps she went, and out across the lawn to the sidewalk, before the screen door could bang shut. There she stopped, turned with hands on her hips, and waited for Bernard who was carrying the big carton of cookies and balancing his skateboard on top.

"Whatcha' bringing that for?" she teased. "You're supposed to help me. Not go skating."

"I'm not going skating. I'm balancing the box on the skateboard so's I don't have to carry it, silly."

"Oh," Mary said, "you're the one who's silly. Silly, silly, silly." Then she bounded down the sidewalk at a skip.

At the very first house, she made an abrupt left

turn and skipped up to the door, ringing the bell. Bernard rolled the skateboard and the box down to the lamp-post in front of the house and waited for her. Suddenly he heard the "pong" of a soccer ball being kicked, and as he turned he saw Turtle, Jo Jo, and Ernie coming up the street toward him, kicking the ball between them. When they saw Bernard they called out, then kicked the ball toward him and followed along at a run. Seeing the ball coming, Bernard moved to it and with a head butt sent it sailing straight up into the sky. Turtle ran in first, catching the ball when it came down.

"Hey Bernard. Want to come practice with us? We could work on that boomerang ball trick.

"Naw, I can't."

"Why not?" Jo Jo asked.

"Cuz."

"Cuz why?" Ernie said, grabbing the ball from Turtle.

"Just cuz."

"Why?" Turtle said, grabbing the ball back.

"Cuz, Mrs. Mueller is making me help Little Mary sell her Girl Scout cookies, that's why."

"What a bummer," Jo Jo exclaimed.

"Really!" Ernie chimed in.

"Oh, it's not too bad. I'm really not selling them, I'm just a kind-of body guard while she sells them."

Little Mary came running from the porch, yelling. "I sold two boxes. I sold two boxes!" She grabbed two from the big carton, then ran back to the house to deliver them.

Turtle squinted down at the open carton. "How many boxes do you have in there"

"Gee, I don't know. This whole case, I guess."

Turtle stooped and counted them. "Only 22 boxes in here. Why don't you just sell them all, then you can come and practice with us"

"Are you kidding? Twenty two boxes. By the time she sells all of those boxes it will be way past bedtime."

Ernie looked in the box." Yep, that's a lot of boxes in there all right."

"Come on you guys, let's go," Ernie said.

"Wait a minute guys." Turtle held up his hand to stop them from going further. "What if we all pitch in and help sell these cookies?"

"What do you mean?" Jojo chimed in.

"All four of us, and Mary," Turtle said. "We could all pitch in and help, then we could sell them five times as fast."

Jo Jo smirked. The corners of his mouth turned up and his eyes twinkled a bit. "Wouldn't we all look kinda' silly selling Girl Scout cookies? He, he, he. I mean, we're not girls."

"Who cares who sells them? Boys can sell stuff too. Come on, you guys. Let's do it."

Bernard looked toward Mary as she came skipping back from the house with the money in her hand. "Well, I'm game if it's okay with Mary. We could ask her."

"I heard you, I heard you, I heard you."

"So, you want us to help, or not?"

"Yes. Yes, yes, yes. Then I can get home in time to watch The Brady Bunch on the TV."

"Great," Turtle said, rubbing his hands together in glee. "This will be great. Let's divide the boxes up. Let's see. Five into twenty two won't come out even, so we'll take four each, and two of us will get one extra box to sell. Okay?"

"I'll take an extra one," Bernard said.

"Me too," Turtle exclaimed happily.

"But, no eating of any of my cookies," Mary chimed in. "No, no, no."

Turtle reached into the big carton and started

laying the boxes out on the sidewalk in even piles. Jo Jo picked up his stack. "How much are these things, anyway?" he said. "And, what do we say when we knock on the door?"

Little Mary looked at him with a big sneer and placed her hands on her hips, saying. "You silly-billy, Jo Jo. The price is right on the box. Two dollars each, and there is a little card on every box telling exactly what to say. Just read it. Silly, silly, silly."

"All right," Bernard said. "But I'll have to stay with Mary, cause Mrs. Mueller said so."

"So, you don't like me," Mary cried, "and that's the only reason. Because Mrs. Mueller told you to?"

"No. Don't be silly. Of course I like you."

"And that's the reason you'll stay with me? Cause you like me?"

"Right. That's the reason. I'll stay with you because I like you, and you are one of my best friends. But also, because Mrs. Mueller asked me to, and I don't want to hurt her feelings by disobeying. Okay?"

"Okay." Mary smiled.

Bernard turned back to the boys, and with a big sigh of relief, continued what he had been saying.

"So," he said, "we'll all take different streets, then meet over by the General Store when we're all done selling the cookies, okay, guys?"

They all agreed, then split up and headed in different directions, down different streets, to sell the cookies.

Turtle took C street, passing the first two houses, then at the third house turned up the wide brick walkway and mounted the porch of a big white house with green roof, shutters, and trim. He knocked on the door.

A large lady in a flowered apron and a hot pad in one hand opened the door and stared down at Turtle over horn-rimmed glasses. She looked shocked and perturbed at seeing him standing there. "What in the world are you doing, Turtle?" she asked.

"I'm practicing being a door to door salesman," he said.

"Oh. And what are you selling?"

"Girl Scout cookies. You see, I'm helping little Mary and Bernard sell these Girl Scout cookies because it's for a very good cause." Turtle pulled out the card and took a big deep breath to begin reading the sales pitch, but before he could even get one word out the woman said, "All right. I'll take two boxes."

"You will?"

"Yes. How much are they?"

"Two dollars a box."

"Fine," she said taking two of the boxes, then dug into her apron pocket and pulled out four one dollar bills. She handed them to Turtle, who stared at them in happy disbelief.

"Gee thanks, Mom," Turtle said as he turned and jumped back off the porch, skipping away.

"Don't be out too late," his mom called out after him before she closed the door.

Sheriff George and Jim were cruising the street in the old police wagon when they noticed Turtle skipping along the sidewalk. It was a pretty funny sight to see, so they just fell in behind him and followed along until he turned up the next sidewalk and knocked on the door to the next house. They waited and watched as Turtle spoke to the old couple who came and opened the door.

Jim looked over at the frown upon the Sheriff's face and noticed by the way his shoulders drooped and the way he held his head that he was disturbed about something.

"You feel all right, Sheriff?" he asked. "I notice that

you seem to be kinda sad looking today."

"Oh? I didn't realize that anyone would notice. How can you tell?"

"Well, I'm kind of a student of body language, you know. That's the science of just looking at people and telling what they are thinking or how they feel."

"Really? I heard about that body language stuff, saw it on the TV. They use it at airports and places to try to spot hijacker and crooks and terrorists, right?"

"That's right. It's gotten to be a real science lately."

"Well, that could come in real handy in police work, I guess."

"So, I can tell the way you hold your head and your body that something is troubling you, Sheriff."

"Yep. You're right as rain. I guess it's because of Snowball."

"Your new cat?"

"Yep. We only had her a few days, and I was getting kinda fond of her, the way she would always greet me with a big meow when I got home, and all. And snuggle up to me and purr when I was home watchin' TV."

"Well, what happened to her?"

"Danged if I know. When I got up this morning, she was just gone. I looked all over for her, but I couldn't find her anyplace."

"Maybe she'll come back. Cats do that, you know. They're pretty independent, and sometimes they go away, they're gone for a while, then they just come back."

"I know that, and I've been hoping that she would. Then again, I thought, maybe she just went back to where she came from. Maybe she has a good home someplace else. Anyway, I kinda miss her."

"Well, I'll surely keep an eye peeled for her, Sheriff, and if I spot her I'll let you know right away."

"You will? Well, you can't miss her, if you see her. She's a tiny little cat and she's all white."

"Well, if I see her, I'll call you right away. You don't have to worry about that. Oh, oh. Looky there. Here comes that little fat boy. He's walking back towards the street."

Sheriff George gave two little light taps to his horn button so that it wasn't enough to disturb anyone in the neighborhood, but just two little beep beeps to get Turtle's attention. But Turtle was so busy counting his money, and walking with his head down that he didn't even hear it, so the Sheriff pulled up right alongside him as he walked along, and yelled "Turtle," right in his ear. Turtle was so surprised that he almost jumped out of his skin. He took two steps away, then fell over a rock and rolled on the lawn.

"Turtle, come over here, please," the Sheriff called out.

"Oh, sure. Hiya Sheriff."

"Have you met my new Deputy, Turtle?

"No. I haven't."

"Well, this is him. Jim Cranberry is his name and he'll be around if you ever need him."

"Hi, Deputy Cranberry."

"Hi, Turtle."

"Say," the Sheriff said cautiously, "you haven't seen a pure white cat around here anyplace by any chance?

"Nope. I sure haven't Sheriff.

"What in the dickens are you up to, Turtle? How come you been knocking on these doors? You selling magazines, or something?"

"Well, no Sheriff, I'm selling Girl Scout cookies.

"Girl Scout cookies?" the Sheriff said, surprised.

"Yep, you see, me and JoJo and Ernie are helping Bernard and Little Mary sell her Girl Scout cookies so we can all finish sooner. Then we can practice some soccer kicks."

"Oh," said the Sheriff, smiling. "I see. Well, that's real nice of you to help Little Mary out like that. As a matter of fact I was kinda lookin' for Bernard to ask him something. Do you know where he is?"

"Well, he's around."

"Around? Well, let me ask the question this way. Do you happen to know where he is, right now?"

"Oh, sure. I do."

"Well, would you mind telling me and Deputy Jim exactly where he is, right now?"

"It isn't illegal to sell Girl Scout cookies without a license in Miners Oaks, is it, Sheriff?"

"No, Turtle. We just want to talk to him."

"Well, he should be up on Main Street by now, just around the corner."

The Sheriff reached back and pushed the rear door of the station wagon open. "Okay, Turtle," he said, "get in the car please and we'll all go see if we can find Bernard, okay?"

Turtle climbed into the back seat of the wagon, and the door slammed shut as the Sheriff put the vehicle into gear and started off down the street.

"Say, Sheriff," Turtle said. How about you and Deputy Jim here buying some of these Girl Scout cookies? The money goes for a very worthwhile cause, you know, they come in different flavors, and they're really delicious too."

Ernie chuckled to himself as the door was closed in front of him, "Wow! What a salesman I am," he muttered out loud. He counted the money twice, then stuffed it into his jeans pocket and walked away down the sidewalk to the curb. There, he stopped, turned back to look at the building where he had just made his very first sale. The big sign over the door read Miners Oaks Bakery. "Wow!" Ernie said out loud. "Anyone who can sell cookies to a cookie factory has got to be the greatest salesman in the world. I think I've found my calling."

Bernard and Little Mary came down the main street to the edge of town, then headed right for the General Store, Mary hobbling along in front, and Bernard pushing the skateboard with the big box on it, following behind.

Directly across the street, in the Seven-Eleven, J.D., Spider, Ugly Joe, Creep and Wimp were playing video games and hanging out when Spider, looked out the window and saw Bernard. He grabbed at J.D.'s arm.

"Hey, J.D. Lookie, lookie, lookie."

"Don't bother me now. I'm almost breaking ten thousand."

"But J.D. It's Bernard."

"Oh yeah? Where?"

They looked just in time to see Bernard and Little Mary disappear into the General Store across the street.

"Okay, you guys. Keep an eye on that door and tell me when he comes out."

The little brass bell clanged loudly as Bernard and Mary entered the old fashioned store and closed the door. It was a place that even a blind man could recognize in his sleep. The smell of it and the feel of being here was like being enveloped in history. This place had been here for over a hundred years, and it was still a place where the old men gathered around the wood burning stove to tell stories and reminisce about the days when the west was wild. The owner of the store had been a boy when his grandfather built it, in the days of the old wild west, and though some reconstruction had been done, it was pretty much as it had been then. The Old Timer, as he was now called, was approaching one hundred and five years of age. Partially blind and very hard of hearing, he still worked every day of his life. Seated now with his feet propped upon the old stove, he didn't hear the bell as it signalled Bernard and Little Mary entering. He sat in the middle of his memorabilia, quietly engrossed in a copy of Arizona Highways.

Bernard, knowing that the old man was hard of hearing, walked around, positioned himself directly in front of the Old Timer and waited patiently for him to look up and focus.

A smile crossed the old man's lips when he saw the two of them standing there.

"Bernard. Mary. Well, hello. Pull up a barrel and sit yourselves down."

"Well, Mr. Old Timer, we can't stay long. We're selling Girl Scout cookies, and we thought you might like some."

The old man reached for his ear horn, to help him hear. It was actually a real horn of a bull that had been hollowed out, with a string put on it so it could be hung on the wall, or around his neck, and a rubber tip on one end so that it wouldn't hurt when he put it in his ear. He put it into his ear now, leaned forward in his chair, and, aiming the wide fluted part at Bernard, said in a high squeeky voice, "What'd you say?"

"I said, Girl Scout cookies," Bernard said more loudly.

"Whaaat?"

"I'm helping the girls," Bernard said motioning toward Mary. "Girls."

"Girls, girls, girls," Mary yelled.

"Squirrels?" the old man said. "No squirrels around here."

"Not squirrels, Mr. Old Timer. GIRLS."

"Squirrels live in the mountains. You have to go up there to find them."

"We know that, sir."

"What would you want with squirrels anyway? You can't keep em' as pets. You can't tame em'. They have fleas, they will bite you, and they don't even taste good."

"No, no, no," Little Mary said, wagging a finger at the old man. Bernard tried to yell even louder at the old man.

"We're helping the Girl Scouts. SCOUTS, SCOUTS."

"Shout? No need to shout. You see, I have this here ear horn so I can hear you. It was made from a real bull's horn."

"Yes, Sir. We know that."

"People are always shouting at me. Can't for the life of me figure out why. Now, what is it that you and little Mary wanted, Bernard?"

"Never mind, Mr. Old Timer," Bernard said as he motioned to Mary for them to leave. Then the old man's eyes lit up.

"Say, what's that you got there in those boxes? Looks like Girl Scout cookies. I love Girl Scout cookies. Can't wait for those cute little darlings to come around every year so I can buy some. Can I get a couple of those boxes from you, Bernard?"

The police wagon with the Sheriff, Jim, and Turtle cruised down the main street looking for Bernard, but passed by the General Store and disappeared around the corner of Broadway just as Bernard and Mary came out.

However, J.D. and Spider, saw them and the gang quickly dropped what they were doing and moved outside to intercept the kids.

"Well, well, lookie lookie lookie. It's Mr. goody goody and his little crippled friend, guys."

"That's not a nice thing to say, J.D.," Bernard said. "It doesn't bother me, but you hurt Mary's feelings when you say things like that."

J.D. laughed, then put on a fake smile and played the part of a polite man, showing off for his gang of ruffians. "Oh, I'm so sorry if I offended you. Bernard. Mary. Please accept my apology."

"Of course. What are you fellas doing over here, anyway? The game isn't 'til Sunday," Bernard said as the gang encircled them, closing in even tighter.

Spider shot a glance at J.D. and laughed an evil laugh, mocking Bernard, "The game isn't 'til Sunday. He, he, he."

Ugly Joe and Creep laughed too, then J.D. moved right close to Bernard and said, "Yeah, we know that the game isn't 'til Sunday. We were just kind of riding around and I said to the guys here, I said, 'I wonder what my old friend Bernard Wheel is doing?' Didn't I fellas?"

The gang all laughed and agreed with J.D.

"Well, that was really nice of you," Bernard said, then Spider cut him off, mimicking him again, "really nice of you."

"What are those boxes you have there?" J.D. asked.

"These? Oh, these are Girl Scout cookies."

"Girl Scout cookies?"

"I'm helping Little Mary here, sell them."

J.D. laughed. "You're selling Girl Scout cookies? Are you a girl, Bernard?"

"No, I'm not a girl. I'm just helping Mary."

J.D. reached out and touched Bernard's jacket,

fingering the material. Then, in a sugary sweet but sinister voice, he hissed. "Do you wear girl's clothes too, Bernard?" Then J.D. deliberately spilled his soft drink on Bernard's jacket.

"Ooooppps, I spilled my drink. Oh, I'm sooo sorry."

"Oh, that's okay J.D. It's a waterproof jacket."

"Waterproof! Gee, ain't that great. Isn't it fellas?" Then J.D. pulled a switchblade knife from his pocket and snapped the blade open right under Bernard's nose." I wonder if it's knife proof, too?"

Little Mary clung tightly to Bernard and started to cry, "I wannna go home, Bernard. Let's go home."

Just then the police wagon rounded the corner behind them, and headed right up to where Bernard and the boys were standing. Wimp saw the police wagon first and nudged Spider, who nudged J.D. and J.D. quickly folded up his switchblade and put it away, while the rest of the gang loosened the circle around Bernard and Mary as the Sheriff pulled up, parked and got out of the car.

"Well, it's been real nice talking to you, Bernard," J.D. laughed. Smiling broadly he started backing away. "See you at the game on Sunday. We gotta split now."

"Hey, wait a minute J.D.," Bernard said. "How about buying some of these Girl Scout cookies? It's for a real worthy cause, they come in different flavors, and they taste real good too."

The Sheriff waved toward J.D. and his group, motioning for them to come back closer. "What are you guys doing all the way over here in Miners Oaks, J.D.?" he asked.

J.D. had to think fast. "Well, I, unh, you see, Sheriff... we... uh, we heard that Bernard was selling Girl Scout cookies, to help Little Mary here out, and they've always been a personal favorite of mine. So we just rode over to get some. Didn't we guys?"

Spider shot a look at Ugly Joe, who looked at Creep, who looked at Wimp, who looked at J.D., then they all shrugged their shoulders and then shook their heads, "Yes."

"Great," Bernard said. "Wow, isn't it a lucky thing that I have just enough boxes for all of you guys?"

The Sheriff scratched his head and watched as the boys all paid Bernard, took their boxes, then mounted their bikes and rode off down Main Street and disappeared into the darkness at the edge of town.

"Seems kinda funny that they would ride all the way over here just for cookies, Bernard."

"Well, they were probably out for a ride, anyway," Bernard said.

"Yeah, well listen Bernard, I asked Turtle about this on the way over here, but he didn't know what it was. I was wondering if you might know." The Sheriff fished the small piece of metal out of his pocket and showed it to Bernard. "You recognize this?"

Bernard took it from the Sheriff's palm, held it up to the light, looked at it closely, then handed it back. "Sure."

"You do? What is it?"

"It's a piece of a Shomuyo brake handle."

"A sho... what? Are you sure?"

"I'm positive. See that little line on the inside edge?" Bernard pointed to the little mark on the metal and the Sheriff looked.

"Yes, but it just looks like a scratch to me."

"Nope. It's not a scratch. It's part of the logo. They stamp it right about there. This is the bottom part of the S. It's a real fancy S with a long tail on the end of it. The rest is broken off, but that's what it is all right."

Jim took the piece from the Sheriff and stared at the place that Bernard had indicated. "Well I'll be doggone and hornswaggled. It does look like part of an S. You can just see where it starts to curve up where it broke off. Funny I never noticed that before."

Sheriff George took it back again, squinting at it more carefully. "I've never heard of this Shim... Shimmm what-o."

"Shomuyo. You say it in three parts. Sho--like show, mu, like a cow going moo, and yo, like in yoyo. Shomuyo. It's a rare Japanese trail bike. They don't make them anymore. I think they were bought out by an American company about three years ago. But lots of kids still use parts from those old bikes. They put them on their new bikes because they are made of a very lightweight metal, and they are great brakes."

"You mean this could have come from any kind of bike?"

"Yep. Or maybe a motor bike, or a go-cart. Lots of people use them."

"Well, I'll be gol-danged, the Sheriff said, handing the piece back to Jim. Get on the phone tomorrow, Jim, see if we can find out who sold these bikes. Get anything on it that you can."

"Yes sir. I surely will."

"Is that all you wanted, Sheriff?" Bernard asked.

"Yes. And thanks Bernard. I appreciate it."

"How come you want to know about Shomoyu?"

"Well, it's part of an investigation me and Jim here are conducting, and I can't really talk about it right now. Say, did you meet my new deputy, Jim Cranberry?"

Jim held out his hand and shook Bernard's. "Very pleased to meet you Bernard. And you too, Little Mary. The Sheriff told me all about you kids, and about your Superbike, Bernard."

"He did?"

"Yep. He said you two kids were the nicest kids in

Miners Oaks, and I can see that he was telling the truth about that, all right."

Just then Ernie and JoJo rounded the corner and called out to Bernard, and Mary, and Turtle from across the street. "We sold em' all," they yelled happily. Bernard and Turtle said goodbye to the Sheriff and Jim, and taking little Mary, each by one hand, they crossed the street to meet their friends. As they all went off down the street, Jim got an envelope from the station wagon, slipped the tiny piece of metal into it, sealed it, then put it in the glove compartment for safe keeping. "A bike, or a go-cart, or a motorbike, or maybe even one of those three wheeled all terrain vehicles."

"Doesn't really narrow the field down much, does it?" the Sheriff said, taking off his big cowboy hat and scratching his head.

"Well, it's better than a poke in the eye with a sharp stick," Jim joked. "At least it eliminates elephants, Big Foot, and water buffalos."

"Ain't that the truth. Well, I'm going home. We'll mull this all over in the morning, and it wouldn't hurt if you kinda took a look out by the Cooper farm tonight. You never know, they just might try to get another cow. And if something should come up, I want you to call me. Don't try to be a hero and get yourself in a jam."

"I surely will Sheriff. If there is any trouble, I surely will. And, I'll keep an eye peeled for that white cat of yours while I'm at it too."

CHAPTER NINE

It was around ten PM when Jim dropped the Sheriff off at his house. George gave him a list of places to check and final instructions, then Jim drove off to do his rounds.

The night sky was dotted with a thousand bright stars all glittering like shiny diamonds in the heavens as the wagon disappeared down the street, and the sheriff walked up the driveway to his house. There was the crunch of the gravel under his black cowboy boots and the songs of crickets filled the air as he passed the front door and walked all the way around to the back. Looking all around, he cupped his hands to his mouth and called out, "Snowball. Here, Kitty, kitty, kitty."

He stood there silently, listening, then the back door opened with a creaking sound and his wife looked out at him.

"I looked all over for her all day, and called out for

her too, but there was no answer," she said.

The Sheriff looked at the far off hills and listened, his ear turned in the hope that he might hear that faint meow but there was only the buzz from the crickets in the trees and the faint sound of a far away coyote howling at the moon.

"Don't worry honey," his wife said. "She'll probably come back."

The Sheriff just looked out at the hills, saying nothing.

"I have some supper on," his wife said. "Why don't you come in and eat something? You must be tired."

"Okay, I am a little tired, and a bit hungry," the Sheriff replied as he followed his wife into the house.

Jim cruised around Miners Oaks for a while but there wasn't much to see. All the stores were closed by nine o'clock and everyone was at home watching TV, or had already gone to bed, so after checking all the doors on Main Street to make certain they were locked, and cruising all the side streets, Jim decided to take a little drive out to the Cooper farm, as the Sheriff had suggested, to see if anything at all was going on out there.

Arriving at the farm, he drove around a bit until he found a little hill where he could park and look down on the pasture. He set the hand brake, turned the key shutting off the engine, turned out the headlights, and settled down to watch. For a while he listened to the radio and gazed at the cows grazing in the pasture below in the moonlight, but pretty soon he yawned, and after a time his head began to droop and nod. He tried to fight the urge to sleep for a while, but eventually the sandman won the battle and he just dozed off.

Suddenly, there was a knock on the driver's side

window and a bright light shining in. Jim jumped awake, startled out of his dreams, and with the windows all fogged up the way they were, he couldn't see who it was at all. Was it one person, or a whole gang? Were they friendly, or not? It was too late to try and call the Sheriff now, although that thought did run through Jim's mind, and the mobile phone was just inches away from his fingertips, but it was definitely too late now, and he was on his own. It was scary, so he drew his pistol slowly and carefully and rolled the window down just enough so that he could peek out through the crack. The cold air from outside flowed in along with a misty fog, chilling his face. The strong smell of wet grass helped to clear his head a little, but with that bright light shining right into his sleep laden eyes he still couldn't see a thing. "Who is it? Who's there?" he said, pointing his 38 calibre police special out through the narrow opening at whoever or whatever was there. "I have a gun," he shouted in a quivering voice.

"Don't shoot," a tiny voice came back. "It's only me, Ginger, Ginger Cooper."

"Golly gee, Miss Ginger," Jim said apologetically. "You almost scared me half to death."

"Sorry. I didn't mean to. Er, can you put that gun away, please?"

"Oh, sure." Jim rolled the window all the way down and put his gun back in its holster, buttoning down the leather strap that held it in. "I was just parked here trying to see if I could see anything going on with your cows, maybe even catch those rustlers right in the act, if we were lucky, that is, but I didn't see anything, and I guess I got kinda sleepy and dozed off."

"Well, you won't be able to see much if you're asleep," Ginger laughed.

"I know. It's embarrassing. I guess I just got bored and I couldn't fight it anymore. I'm not used to staying up this late. Normally, I'm a day person."

"Me too," Ginger said. "Anyway, just about anybody could see you parked up here on this hill in plain sight, and this old woody wagon stands out like a sore thumb. You need to go around the other side and park behind those trees, out of sight, if you ever expect to catch anybody."

"Oh, yeah, that sounds like a good idea. Okay, I can do that. That's a very good idea, Ginger. Thanks."

"If you'll let me in, I'll ride over there with you and show you the best place to park," Ginger said. "I could even keep you company for a while, so you don't fall asleep."

"Good idea. Well, hop in then, and you can show me how to get over there."

Jim pushed the passenger side door open and Ginger went around and slid in.

"What's that you're wearing?"

"Oh, it's my bathrobe, silly. It's just what I was wearing. I was watching TV and fell asleep, when you honked your horn and woke me up. It's a good thing that Grandpa had gone to bed and sleeps soundly. He might have come out here with a gun and mistaken you for a mountain lion, or something."

"My horn honked? Gosh, I must've hit it when I fell asleep. Funny it didn't wake me up. I must've been really out of it."

"Don't worry," Ginger said. "I'll keep you awake now."

"Gosh, Miss Ginger, you don't know how much I appreciate this."

"Think nothing of it," Ginger said. "After all, it's our cows that you're protecting."

CHAPTER TEN

Bernard was up early in the morning, dressed, ate, and was out the door on a run. He got Superbike, lashed his books to the back with a big rubber band, then took off into the hills on his way to school.

It was a beautiful morning for a ride. The kind that makes you want to take your time, breath the clear mountain air, enjoy the smell of the newborn wild flowers, listen to the birds sing, and enjoy the warmth of the morning sunshine and the big blue cloudless sky.

As Bernard topped the path at Rustler's Ridge he saw Hal sitting on a rock just looking out over the valley below. Senor Birdy was on his shoulder. "Awk! Bernard's here. Bernard's here," Birdy squawked, then took off straight up, flying higher and higher until he disappeared completely in the blazing blue.

"Hi Bernard," Hal said, waving. "Good morning. On your way to school?"

"Yep," Bernard said, stopping his bike. "I can't visit though because if I do I'll be late, and I'm late a lot."

Bernard cupped his hand over his forehead to block the sun and peered all around the sky looking for Senor Birdy, but he didn't see him. "Where'd he go?" Bernard asked.

"Oh, he's just getting a little morning exercise, I guess. He'll be back in a minute."

Then Senor Birdy appeared, coming fast over the trees along the ridge in the distance, and swooping right over Hal and Bernard's heads he let out a big, "Sqwaaak," zooming so close that a blast of air hit them as he passed, then zoomed around in a big circle and went out of sight over the top of the mountain.

"Wow!" Bernard said. "He can really fly fast, and he's like some kind of stunt pilot the way he goes."

"Yep," Hal agreed. "He doesn't usually fly like that. He's happy to see you, and showing off for you, Bernard. Because he likes you."

"I like him too," Bernard said, scanning the sky. Then, as they watched, Senor Birdy came sailing in, very slowly, and spread his wings way out so that he lit, light as a feather, right on Hal's shoulder. A perfect landing. This time though, Bernard noticed that Senor Birdy had a beautiful flower held carefully in his beak."

"Well, who is this for?" Hal asked.

"Aawwkk. Bernard. Tweet, tweet," Birdie said softly.

"For me, Birdy?" Bernard said, surprised. "Gee thanks. I don't know what to say."

"You're welcome. Awk. Tweet, tweet."

"I told you he likes you," Hal said.

"Awwk! I like Bernard. For sure, Tweet. "

"This is really neat," Bernard said. "I'll put it on my desk at school, and later I'll press it in my book and use it as a bookmark."

"Tweet. Good idea, Bernard."

"But, I have to go now or I'll be late for school," Bernard said. "Everyone is always scolding me for being late. Mrs. Mueller, and Coach Bob, and even Mr. Brown. It's a bad habit that I'm trying to get rid of."

"If you want," Hal said slowly, "I can help you with that. I can show you a little trick that will help you so that you'll never be late again."

"Really?" Bernard said.

"Really," Hal repeated.

Senor Birdy ruffled up his feathers and mimicked Hal, "Awk. Really. Tweet."

"Wow, that would be really great. Can you show me the trick right now?"

"I could," Hal said, "but it takes about fifteen minutes to show it to you, and if I did, then you would be late for school."

Birdy chirped, "You'd be late, awwk, learning how not to be late. Awk."

"Gosh, that's right," Bernard agreed.

"But I'd be glad to show you the trick when you have more time. It all has to do with what I told you before about mind over matter. Do you remember that?"

"Oh sure. Yes, I do, and I'm going to try it after school today."

"It will help you with a lot of things, Bernard. Believing in yourself can solve many problems in this world, but you'd better get on to school now, and Birdy and I will see you later. Maybe even after school today."

"Okay, I'd better go now. I'm probably already late."

"You won't be late," Hal said. "You can ride faster than ever before, and you'll be on time."

"Well, bye," Bernard said, waved, and pushed off riding on down the path toward school. The wind seemed strong in his face, and he seemed to be coasting just a little faster than usual, and while he was riding, Bernard kept hearing Hal's last words, remembering what Hal had said. As he rode over the top of the ridge at Blueberry Summit, and started down the other side, he tuned his mind, as Hal had told him to do, and a sudden burst of energy filled his heart. He started pumping on the pedals just a little bit harder, speeding up. This would be a good time to try Hal's lesson out, he thought, as he zoomed faster and faster down the slope.

Not far ahead, J.D. and the gang were hiding in the bushes by the trail, waiting to ambush Bernard on his way to school.

"This is the place," J.D. said. "That little fink always comes this way. Hide the bikes over there, guys. Spider, help me bend this tree branch down."

"We're gonna be late for school, J.D." Spider moaned.

"So, we'll be a little late. So what! Big deal! This won't take long, then we'll take the shortcut. Get hold of this branch. Help me bend it."

"Okay, J.D. But why are we bending this tree? I thought we were going to catch Bernard and beat him up."

"Not beat him up, dummy. Everyone would know we did it and then they wouldn't let us play in the game on Sunday. What we are going to do is arrange an accident. Get on the end of this limb. Give us a hand, Joe."

All three of the boys put their weight on the tree, bending the limb way back. "That's it!" J.D. said breathlessly. "Now, you guys hold it there while I tie it down."

Joe sat on a nearby rock and watched with interest as he munched on a vanilla Girl Scout Cookie. "So what are you tying this tree down for, J.D.? Are you afraid that it will run away? Get it? Run away. He, he, he."

"Not funny Ugly. Now listen to me, here's the plan. Bernard will be coming down the trail this way. I'll go up on the bluff there, and when I see him coming, I'll whistle like a bird, once, like this: 'Tweet' You hide down there, Spider. Take your knife and get ready. Then, when Bernard is right near the tree, I'll whistle twice, like this: 'Tweet, tweet.' Then, when you hear the double whistle, cut the rope."

"Then what, J.D.?"

"Then," J.D. said in a very exasperated voice, "the tree limb will spring back and knock him coo coo."

"Coo coo?"

"Coo coo, means it will knock him silly. Harm him badly, hurt him severely. Maybe even bust his nose or his face. Then, we'll just get on our bikes and ride away. Get it?"

"Okay," Spider said. "Sounds good to me."

"Good plan," Joe said, wiping the crumbs of his last cookie from his mouth. "You got any cookies left J.D?"

"No I don't," J.D. snapped at him. "Now take your positions. I'm going up on the knoll. Wait for my signal, and cut the rope when you hear the two bird whistles."

As J.D. scrambled up to the knoll, Spider took his position by the rope, holding his knife in readiness. Wimp and Joe, with nothing much to do, just sat under a tree and slowly ate the last of their cookies.

As Bernard came to the level spot at the bottom of the path, he spied a little rise just ahead, and as he pumped up to speed with all his might, a sudden blur of color flashed past him. It was a moment or two before he realized that it was Senor Birdy flying over his head. Zooming forward along the path, Birdie glided through the trees, then darted away and disappeared over the hill.

Seeing Birdy gave Bernard extra energy and even more resolve, and when he hit the top of the rise, he pulled back on the handlebars and Superbike zoomed skyward.

J.D spotted Bernard coming and gave the first signal with a loud whistle. "Tweet." Then he saw Bernard jump and his mouth dropped open and his eyes got wide with amazement. He'd never seen anyone on a bike jumping that high or that far before, and he sat transfixed as Bernard flew right by him, high in the air like some silent airplane, vanishing from J.D.'s sight behind some trees, still flying. J.D. slid down the knoll and ran out into the path following in Bernard's direction, to try and see where he'd gone. Just as he did this, a happy mockingbird in a nearby treetop whistled twice to it's mate, "Tweet, tweet," and Spider cut the rope.

"POW!" The tree sprang back, slamming right into J.D's face, knocking him down in a cloud of dust on the path.

"Did we get him?" Ugly Joe called out as he and Spider and Joe ran out into the trail to take a look.

"Somebody get me outa here," J.D. called from underneath the pile of leaves and tangled limbs. "Get me outa' here!"

"I guess we got him," Spider said.

"Now what do we do?" asked Ugly Joe.

"We get on our bikes and ride away," Wimp said. "That's what J.D. told us to do."

"Okay, let's go to school," Spider said, and they all mounted their bikes and rode away.

CHAPTER ELEVEN

Sheriff George was making a fresh pot of coffee as Deputy Jim came into the office around eleven AM. "You're an hour early, he said, looking at his watch."

"Yep, well I had nothing to do so I thought I might as well get started. I picked up the mail at the post office for you, Sheriff. And lookie here. Here's that report from the Police Lab over in Flagstaff on that plaster cast we made out at the Cooper Farm the other day." Jim opened it and started reading it to himself. "Hmmmm. Hmmmm. Very interesting."

"Well, don't keep me in suspense. What does it say?"

"Well sir, it identifies the tire track all right. It says right here in this letter that they had a real hard time because it was such a small section, and that after searching all known records of manufacturers in the U.S. and Canada and finding nothing at all, they searched manufacturers from all over the world."

"Very thorough of them," the Sheriff took a sip of his coffee. "And?"

"Then," Jim continued, "they finally found out that only one manufacturer in the whole wide world has that particular configuration of tire tread, and so, after careful testing and comparison, there is absolutely no doubt as to it's origin."

"Great! Now, are you going to tell me what kind of a tire it is, or are you going to keep me in suspense?"

"Well, yes sir. I was getting to that part."

"Well, get to it."

"Yes sir. Well, it says right here that this particular tire was made in Japan, and is a very popular tire."

"I was afraid of that."

"Yep, They use them on bicycles, mostly trail bikes. Some motorcycles even use them. The so-called HOG motorcycles--the kind the Hell's Angels use."

"Yes, I know, go on."

"Those ones with the big back tire and the itty-bitty front tire."

"Jim. Are you gonna tell me what kind of a tire it is, or would you like your coffee in your lap?"

"Well, sure Sheriff, that is...of course."

"Well, tell me. Tell me, and tell me NOW!"

"Yes sir. It says right here that it's a Kurisaki, 20 X 1.75."

"A bike tire?"

"Yes sir, that's what it is all right, a bike tire."

"Well, that gives us something to go on. I think we'd better go over to the school and take a look at all the bikes."

"Which school Sheriff? There are three or four that I know of and bike racks with lots of bikes in all of them."

"Yep, but we have to start somewhere, and we just

might find a bike out there with this brand of tire, and maybe a broken handle from a Shimoso brake."

"Er, I think it's Shomuyo, Sheriff. Show, moo, yo. Remember how Bernard told us to say it?"

"Right. Whatever. Anyway, it might give us some kind of a lead."

"But, the brake and the tire might not even be on the same vehicle, and both may have nothing at all to do with the rustling."

"I know that, but we have to do something. You got any other clues or better ideas?"

"Well, no sir. Can't say that I do."

The telephone rang interrupting their conversation and Jim being the closest, answered it.

"Hello. Oh, hi Mr. Cooper. No kidding? Another cow gone? Huh? Well, sure. The Sheriff and I will come right out. Don't touch anything. There might be some clues out there. Right. Goodbye."

"Another cow gone?"

"That's what he said."

"Didn't you take a cruise out there last night, like I told you?"

"Well, yes sir, I did, but I didn't see nothing happen."

"Well, let's take a ride over to the school and take a look at the bikes on our way out to the ranch, while the kids are still in their classes. No sense in making waves until we find something definite to go on."

"Right."

Bernard's class was held in a very large airy room with big windows looking out over the soccer field. Bernard looked out just in time to see Coach Bob out there shooing some stray cows off the grass. They did that sometimes, because the grass was so green and perfect there, and Coach Bob was always getting the fences mended and chasing them away, and then cleaning up the field so that the Blue Angels could practice after school, but the cows always came back when nobody was around. It was kinda funny to watch him running around after the cows because the cows didn't want to go and would try to turn back around and run back on the field when Bob chased them. It was a very funny sight to watch.

Mr. Brown tapped on his desk with a ruler and Bernard and all the other kids who were looking out the windows turned straight forward in their seats to listen to him. Then, Mr. Brown went right over to the windows and turned the blinds up so that there was plenty of light in the room but you couldn't see out. He knew that nobody could really concentrate on what he was saying while Coach Bob was out there chasing those cows around.

Mr. Brown was a nice man. He was young and the boys all liked him. Some of the girls even had a crush on him because he was tall and kinda good looking. He looked like a TV star or some kind of sports hero, and he had a real nice and friendly smile. "Now, boys and girls," he said going to the blackboard. "I want to discuss something of great interest." Mr. Brown always said that to get the boys and girls interested, even though some of the stuff that he taught wasn't really that interesting. Taking the eraser, he cleaned the board off, then he wrote a big long word on the blackboard with some white chalk that squeeked as he wrote: L E V I T A T I O N. Then, he turned to the class and smiled that big movie star smile of his, and said, "Can anyone in the class pronounce this word?"

Bernard was the only one to put his hand up and Mr. Brown pointed to him, and Bernard said, "Le-vi-ta-tion."

"Very good Bernard, and can you tell the class

what this word means?"

"Er, I think it means to float in the air, or something like that," Bernard said.

"Right. You are 99% correct. Actually the definition, according to the New Webster's dictionary is, 'to rise or float in the air, allegedly through some supernatural power that overcomes the force of gravity.' Now how many of you here in class actually believe that this is possible?"

A few of the kids raised their hands hesitantly. Mr. Brown pointed to Turtle, who hadn't raised his hand. "You don't think that it is possible, Turtle?"

"Well, gee, Mr. Brown, I don't know. Maybe. I'm not really sure."

"How many are not sure?" Mr. Brown asked and most of the kids raised their hands. "Now we get to the part that makes you really think about things, and that's what I want you to do. I want you to all ask yourselves, is this really possible? And if it is possible, why have we never seen anyone levitate? except in a magic show? And, if it isn't possible, why would we have a word for it in the dictionary? Some very smart men made up this word, used letters to spell it, and put it in the dictionary so we would all know how to say it. Why would they do that if there was no such thing? Now, boys and girls I want you all to realize that one hundred years ago people didn't believe that it was possible to fly. If you could go back to your great-great-grandfather's day and tell him that we could use the telephone to call all around the world, they would think you were crazy. They didn't believe you could send pictures around the world on television, and lot's of other things that we accept now as perfectly natural. So this is your homework assignment for tomorrow, to write a one or two page essay on levitation and give us all your thoughts on this subject."

Bernard raised his hand.

"Yes, Bernard."

"Does this have anything to do with mind over matter?"

"Aha! A very good question. There are those who believe that anything that you can dream or think can be made into reality. That is a very good point. This could possibly make levitation possible, if you believed it strongly enough, according to the theory."

The clang of the school bell resounded throughout the halls, and made the loose window pane in the transom in Mr. Browns classroom vibrate, as it always did. An out of tune jangle matching the melodious ring of the bell in symbiotic harmony. "There is the bell for the assembly. Form a line boys and girls and follow me."

"Testing.. testing... 1.2.3.," they all heard as they walked along the sidewalk between the buildings in double file. Betty Arnett walked next to Bernard and he noticed that she kept giving him these big googly eyes looks as they walked and would turn her eyes away and look down at the ground when he looked back, but he tried to ignore it. He had no idea why she was doing that. Then, they rounded the corner onto the baseball field and saw that a table and chairs had been set up near the cafeteria and Mr. Popoff was there in the middle at a big silver microphone on a stand, and he was talking into it while Mrs. Walker, the music teacher, was trying to adjust the controls. There was a big electronic squeek and screech which made everyone jump, until Mrs. Walker got the volume just right. Mr. Popoff smiled. He had perfectly white teeth, and his head was as round and black as a bowling ball with absolutely no hair on top, and it glistened in the morning sunshine like a Christmas tree ornament. He tapped the microphone a couple of times with his finger then said, "Hello, hello, hello, that's good."

Mr. Brown marched his class into their section of folding seats that had been set up for them, and all the other classes took their places too, and when the whole school was there and seated, Mr. Popoff raised his hand for quiet and all the gibbering and jabbering stopped and a hush came over the group. It was so quiet you could hear the birds singing in a far away tree, and the moo of a cow in a nearby pasture. "Boys and girls of Miners Oaks Elementary School, and fellow teachers," Mr. Popoff said. "I want to thank each and every one of you for giving me one of the very best years that I have ever had in the school system. It has been enlightening, educational, and a pure joy to work with you all this year. Thank you all very much."

There was a smattering of applause by the teachers, then the students joined in. When it was quiet again, Mr. Popoff said, "We are gathered here today to give the annual scholarship awards to those students who have achieved the highest level for their classes and subjects this year, and let me say that you all deserve recognition for a job well done."

Standing behind his class, Mr. Brown shot a glance to the side and seeing something there, moved off into the crowd, unnoticed by his class. At the back of the crowd, over by the fence, he met Mrs. Mueller. "I'm so glad you could make it," Mr. Brown said.

"Are you kidding? I wouldn't have missed this for the world. Does Bernard know?"

"No. I wanted it to be a surprise."

"Oh, I'm so excited. I brought my camera."

"If you stand over here on the side in the back, you can see it all and he won't even have to know that you are here."

Mr. Brown then led her to a place in the back

where she could see everything without being seen.

Mr. Popoff's white shirt glistened and glowed in the bright sunlight as he stood at the microphone. "So now I will announce the scholarship achievement awards for the sixth grade, for best student of the year. When you hear your name please come up and get your certificate. In Mr. Brown's class... and this award goes to Bernard Wheel."

Mrs. Mueller's heart went thump and she put her hand up to her mouth to suppress the sound of her deep sigh. She could see Bernard seated just ahead of her in the seats and watched him look around in amazement. Turtle, seated beside him gave him a push and Bernard got up slowly, then walked to the podium and went up beside Mr. Popoff as the audience applauded and cheered. Mr. Popoff gave him the wooden plaque and pushed him up to the microphone and stepped back a bit so that Bernard could say something.

"Well, gee..." Bernard said, he was a little shocked to hear his own voice resound around the quadrangle over the speakers, but he continued. "I just like to study. It's fun, and Mr. Brown makes it so easy... and fun.. and he answers all our questions and stuff, and I guess he should get all the credit. Gee, thanks. It's a really neat thing, and I'll hang it on my wall in my room where I can look at it every day. Thanks."

The crowd applauded and Bernard made his way down off the platform and through the crowd, moving back toward his seat. It wasn't until then that he saw Mrs. Mueller and Mr. Brown coming toward him. She took him in her arms and gave him a big kiss on the forehead, and a big hug. Tears were streaming down her face, making Bernard's neck wet, but he didn't mind.

"Oh, I'm so proud of you, Bernard," she said. Stand over there with Mr. Brown, please. I want to take your picture, the two of you together. And hold that award in front of you so I can get it all in the picture. That's good. Now smile. Say, cheese."

Bernard held up the plaque and Mr. Brown put his arm around him, while Mrs. Mueller focused, then Bernard saw someone in the crowd behind her, way off in the back. It was Hal, and Hal waved and smiled. Then the flash of the camera blinded him for a second, and when he blinked and re-focused his eyes, and looked again, Hal wasn't there anymore. He had just disappeared.

At that very moment, Sheriff George and Deputy Jim were on the other side of the school near the bike racks, unseen by anyone at the award ceremony. They walked along the bike racks, looking closely at all of them. The Sheriff went one row, while Jim walked along the other.

"See anything, Jim?" the Sheriff asked.

"Nope, got two bikes with Shomoyo brake handles, but no broken ones, and no Kurisaki tires. It's a big zero."

"It could mean that they replaced the handle, or changed tires."

"I don't think so. I checked to see if either of them looked like they had been changed, and it didn't look like it to me. No scratches or anything on them and they all look pretty old. How about over there?"

"I checked every bike. I didn't find any brake handles or Kurisaki tires in that bunch."

"Well, this isn't the only school hereabouts. Maybe we are just checking at the wrong school."

"Yep. Well, we better get on out to the Cooper place and look around. Maybe we'll find some new clues out there that will help us with this. Say, are you coming to the soccer game this Sunday, Jim?"

"I heard about it, and I sure would like to come."

"As a matter of fact, we might even need another referee for that game. Do you know anything about soccer?"

"I sure do. I played myself when I was a kid and I was assistant coach for a team over in Flagstaff a couple of years ago."

"Well golly gee, Jim. That's great. I'm a referee you know, and we surely could use your help, and by the way, if we are both there we will have an opportunity to keep an eye peeled for any bike or motorcycle that might fit our clues. There'll be a lot of them there on Sunday for sure."

"Right, of course, it might be an all-terrain vehicle or a go-cart, or maybe even a wheel barrow."

"But not an elephant, or a water buffalo."

CHAPTER TWELVE

Friday was a busy day for Bernard. First there was school, then he rode home for dinner, then all the way back to school for soccer practice, and after that he took a ride through the forest looking for Hal and Birdy. He had tried to find them the day before, on Thursday, but somehow couldn't find the path that he had taken before, and it started getting dark, so he just went home.

Thursday night, however, he had a dream, and in the dream he was lost in the forest and some monsters were chasing him, but just as the monsters were about to catch him and eat him up, Hal ran up and chased them all away. Then, just as he was about to thank Hal for saving him, he turned around and Hal and Birdy had just disappeared. Now he wanted to find Hal and tell him about the dream, so he rode up and down all the forest trails looking for that path that led to the clearing until he was all tired out and the light was beginning to fade.

Then, just as he was about to give up and go home, he heard a "Squaaak!" coming from behind some trees. He rode in that direction, and when he rounded a corner in the trail, there was Hal, sitting in a clearing by a small campfire, and Birdy was perched nearby on a tree limb.

"Wow!" Bernard said, all out of breath, "I've been looking all over for you guys, and I almost got lost in the forest."

"Well, come sit here by the fire, Bernard. Take a little rest before you go home. I was just fixing something to eat. Would you care for something?"

"Awwk! Hi, Bernard. Tweet."

"Hi Birdy. No thanks, Hal. Mrs. Mueller fixed me supper before soccer practice and I'm not hungry at all."

"Not even for a cookie?" Hal said, extending a stick that had a big brown sweet smelling ball on the end of it.

"You can make cookies over a campfire?" Bernard asked, astonished.

"Awk! Tweet. It's a cookie. It's a cookie."

"Try it." Hal said wiggling the stick in front of Bernard's nose so that the smell of it enticed him. Bernard pulled the cookie off of the stick and bit into it. "Wow! he exclaimed. That's the best cookie I ever tasted in my whole entire life. Even better than Mrs. Mueller makes. How did you do that?"

"Well, thanks for the compliment, Bernard, but it's a family secret that I have sworn never to tell. Want another one?"

"Well, sure. Gee, I didn't think it was even possible to make cookies over a campfire."

Hal laughed. "Everything is possible, if you believe that it is," Hal said, pushing the stick through another tender morsel and passing it over to Bernard, who disposed of it in one scrumptious bite.

"I had a dream," Bernard said while chewing, "and

in this dream monsters were after me and you and Birdy chased them away. Isn't that kinda weird?""

"No. You see, dreams are just your mind sorting things out while you sleep. It's a good dream, Bernard," Hal said.

"But what does it mean?"

"Well, I think that it means only that you are searching for answers and truth, and there are things that you think are keeping you from it. Some things represent other things."

"So the monsters are those other things?"

"Right, they represent curtains blocking your view, preventing knowledge from coming in, and since Birdy and I have taught you a couple of simple little things, you see us as kind of pulling back those curtains for you, or chasing away the monsters. It was a good dream, Bernard. It means you are learning and the more you learn, the more you want to learn."

"One thing that I really want to learn, and I never can, is where I came from, and who my parents really are."

"You will learn all that someday, Bernard. But right now you must learn who you are, and what your life purpose is. Without that knowledge, it makes no difference where you came from, or who your father and mother are."

"But how will I ever learn, what you said, who I really am, and, and...?"

"What your purpose in life is? Well, that is everyone's problem, and we all have to solve it for ourselves. That is our quest in life, and you start by taking one small step in that direction, and you keep on taking those steps until you find the answer. There is no one answer." Hal reached into his pocket then and when he pulled his hand out again it was balled up in a fist. He extended his arm and hand toward Bernard, then opened his hand slowly, palm up, and there in his hand was a small, smooth, stone. "This is a special little stone," Hal said. "Take it and keep it in your pocket always, and when you need an answer to any question, ask this stone."

Bernard took the stone from Hal's hand and looked at it closely. It was kind of flat, about as big and as thick as a checker piece, but smooth as glass and oval shaped around the edges, and it was a very pretty blue color. "You mean this stone can answer any question I ask it?"

"Not all questions, Bernard. And sometimes it takes a while for the answers to come. Sometimes you have to ask the stone the same question many times, but one day, a little voice inside your head will come and it will tell you the answer. Sometimes the answer will not be the one that you want. Sometimes the answer will be that you are asking the wrong question, but you will always get an answer."

"Tweet! Awk! tweet tweet. It's getting late. Mucho tarde," Birdy squawked.

"You'd better go home now, Bernard. It's getting dark, and the trail could be dangerous at night, so be very careful to ride only in the light places."

Bernard was still staring at the stone. It seemed to glow that blue color and it changed shades in the light so that it was hard to take your eyes off of it. Then, when he finally did look up, the campfire was out, and Hal and Birdy were nowhere to be seen, so Bernard just put the stone in his Blue Angel's jacket pocket, got on Superbike, and started out for home.

CHAPTER THIRTEEN

It was an icy clear night, and the big yellow moon cast its golden image upon the face of the shimmering lake as Bernard rode home. There, in the sparkling blue waters, the moon drops danced and shattered, then sped away, disappearing into the blackness of the forest at the rocky shores of Lake Madera Azul.

Night birds sang, courting their mates, and fluffy old owls watched from high borne trees as the nocturnal things left their daytime covers.

The prey and the predators were hidden there, in the dark recesses of the leaves and trees. The squirrels and the coyotes, the spiders and the mosquitos, and in one tiny corner of the thicket, five young boys, J.D. and his gang, waited in hiding to try and get even with Bernard for reasons even they didn't fully understand.

One smattering of fractured moonbeam illuminated the silver-like thread of piano wire that J.D. had strung, neck high, across the bicycle path. So very pretty in this light, but like a spider's web, so very deadly. Barely visible in the dark, it waited for its victim to arrive.

Surely, Bernard would not be able to see it, as he raced his Superbike pell-mell down the steep and twisting mountain path at full speed toward this silent executioner.

There was no reason to suspect a trap, and Bernard's mind was locked in a dream. His life was making twists and turns now. Moments of inspiration. Flashes of understanding, and thoughts that he had never ever experienced before. His life was changing rapidly. New little mental doors were opening. New plateaus. Opportunities to find out who he really was, and more importantly, why? He was twelve years old, and every second of living seemed to bring a brand new adventure. Now, as he rode with the wind in his face, the trees whizzing by in one continuous blur, Superbike and he seemed to be bonded together as if they were one, as if they were flying. So while his body rode, his mind wandered elsewhere. Thoughts of Hal, the mysterious stranger that he had met in the forest, raced by. Images of Senor Birdy. Thoughts of Mrs. Mueller, and of his teacher, Mr. Brown, and of all his friends, mixed with feelings of floating endlessly and effortlessly in space. All these revolved and melted together in a sort of crazy daydream, like previews of a dozen movies all going in his head at once.

Then, suspended in this fantasy void, he imagined that he heard someone call his name. "Bernard," the voice boomed.

"Shall I answer?" was his first thought, then, "Don't be silly," he told himself. "How could anyone know my name out here in space? Could it be my father? No, of course not." Especially not his father, because he would not even know what he was called now, because Bernard had picked out his own name.

Bernard knew that he had an unusual name. And it was fun to see people's eyes get real wide with wonder the very first time that they heard it, and then they would say the name back to him with kind of a funny expression on their faces:

"Bernard Wheel? What an unusual name." And though this had happened many times, Bernard always hoped that one day someone would say, "I know a man with that name, and then Bernard would be able to find out who he really was, and who and where his real father was.

Spider peered down the trail and saw Bernard coming, then hissed, "Pssst! J.D., he's coming now."

J.D. peered over the top of a bush and saw that Bernard was indeed coming down the trail.

"Don't you think this is a little radical?" Ugly Joe said. "I mean, I don't mind hurting the dude, but the piano wire will..."

"Shut up," J.D. snarled. "I'm the boss of this gang and what I say goes. Now sit down and shut up. I don't want him to hear us."

Superbike's wheels made a swooshing noise as they glided along through the fallen leaves that were strewn along the pathway. Bernard thought of the rock in his pocket, and he slowed, and pulled up to a stop at the highest part of the trail where he could see the whole lake below shimmering in the moonlight. He took the rock out of his pocket and looked at it. The way it glowed in the yellow light was really a sight to see, then he said to it, "Which is the fastest way home?"

The rock looked pretty, but no answer came to Bernard's mind as he looked over the terrain ahead, so he slid the stone back into his pocket. "Well," he said to himself, "if you won't tell me, I'll just take the path that has the most moonlight, and that would be this way." Then he turned Superbike and rode down the steep embankment to the lake's edge, and then rode along the bank to the other side, and off through the trees toward Miners Oaks.

"Where'd he go?" J.D. said, looking around and not seeing Bernard. "He should have been here by now."

"Look," Spider said. "There he goes, way on the other side of the lake. He went another way."

"But he always goes this way," J.D. said in disgust.

"Well, he didn't this time," Ugly Joe said.

"I'm kinda glad he didn't," Wimp murmured so nobody could hear. "I didn't want to kill anybody."

"What did you say?" J.D. snarled.

"Nothing," Jimbo said. "Not a thing."

"Okay, you guys, let's get this piano wire down, and get out of here." Then J.D. reached for the wire and let out a holler. "Ooooch," he said, "a darn spider bit me."

"Doggone," Ugly Joe said. "You sure do have some bad luck, J.D. Well, at least it wasn't a poisonous one."

"Shut up and help me with this wire," J.D. said.

CHAPTER FOURTEEN

Sunday started out like any other morning. The rooster crowed and the sun rose in a shimmering red ball, melting the fragrant dew from the flowers and drying the grass, leaving the air smelling pure and sweet. The church bells began ringing as usual at exactly seven a.m. and after the eight o'clock and the nine o'clock services were over, most of the men of Miners Oaks changed into their work clothes and started heading for the field by the school, to get the field ready for the game. They had all worked very hard the day before, setting up the stands and the booths, but there was still much more to do. First, they had to chase all the cows out of the pasture, then get the field cleaned up and ready. Deputy Jim went around with a scoop and a wheelbarrow, picking up everything he could find, while Sheriff George got out the chalk wagon and started making the white lines that marked the playing field borders. He was walking along, pushing that old cart, with the big iron wheels squeeking as he went, when suddenly he stopped, let out a kind of low groan, and lifted one foot up, standing like a big Flamingo bird balancing on one leg, looking at his boot. "Hey, Jim," he called out, "Over here. You missed one."

Mr. Cooper and Turtle's dad were stringing up banners while Mr. Bascom, the service station man, was filling up balloons from a helium tank and hanging them all around, so that before very long the place began to look more like a circus or a carnival than a cow pasture, and the smell of cotton candy and hot dogs, and popcorn filled the air.

Turtle's dad was up on the top of a tall ladder tying one end of a string of balloons to a pole when J.D. and his gang came zooming in from Devlin Corners on their bikes. They raced in at full speed, weaving in and out of the crowd. Spider almost ran into an old lady, but swerved at the last second and went right under the ladder that Mr. Turtle was standing on, bumping it just a little causing it to wobble. It scared Mr. Turtle so that he had to hang onto the pole to keep from falling. "Crazy kids," he yelled out as the gang roared on through the crowd, around one of the booths, and out into the parking area.

The school bands from both Miners Oaks and Devlin Corners had arrived and started to practice. They made so much noise that they scared all the birds and rabbits and prairie dogs away. You could hear them all the way into town, which made even more people come out to see what was going on.

Sheriff George and Deputy Jim finished their work on the field and came in to take a stroll through the crowd, checking things out. "Wow," Jim commented, "they really decorated this old field up really nice."

"Yep," the Sheriff agreed. "This is just about the

biggest thing to happen in Miners Oaks since the big gold strike way back in 1876."

"And look," Jim said, pointing. "They even have a hot dog stand, and they have those real big fat ones there. Boy, I haven't had one of those for a long time. It sorta makes my mouth water just to smell that juicy dog."

"Me too," the Sheriff agreed. "Let's just get us one." So, they both went to the booth, got their hot dogs and then piled them high with all of the condiments. Jim was just about to take a big bite when he noticed a really pretty girl walking right toward him. She just kept smiling and walking straight at him and Jim couldn't figure out why. When she got real close she said, "Hi there," rolling her big eyes at him and breathing right into his face. Her perfume was sweet, and she was so beautiful that Jim's eyes got real wide and he was so surprised that he just stood there frozen. Then the hot dog and all that relish and mustard and onions and ketchup and mayonnaise just slid out of the bun and right down the front of his shirt.

"It's me," the girl said. "Ginger Cooper."

"Well, golly gee," Jim said, trying to wipe his shirt and badge clean." Gosh, I didn't recognize you in that dress, Miss Cooper. Gee, you look... older... nice, prettier than I've ever seen you. I didn't even recognize you."

"Well thank you, Jimmmee. I made this dress myself," Ginger giggled, posing and turning around to show it all to him. "Grandpa thinks it's a bit racy, but you like it, don't you?"

"Well, yes." Jim stuttered. "I surely do. It's...nice."

"Did you just come to see the game, or are you on duty, or something?"

"Yes. Well, actually, both. You see, me and the Sheriff are kind-of on duty, and we're going to help referee too."

"Oh, well then I guess I'll be seeing you later then,

maybe. I mean if you're not busy or anything after the game."

"Well no. I'm not busy after the game. I mean, after we get all the equipment put away and stuff."

"Well then, maybe I'll see you after the game?"

"Sure thing. We could go get an ice cream, or something."

"I'd like that. Well, bye then. Til later." Ginger waved and walked away as Jim watched. He seemed frozen, like a statue until the Sheriff spoke. "Come on Jim, let's go get changed into our referee uniforms and get the equipment ready."

"Huh? Oh, sure enough Sheriff," Jim said, trying to follow George without taking his eyes off of Ginger, but he failed to see the pile of cardboard boxes nearby and stumbled and fell over them. Embarrassed, he picked himself up as fast as he could, then ran quickly after Sheriff George.

CHAPTER FIFTEEN

Mrs. Mueller was scurrying about the kitchen, packing a picnic lunch and trying to get the kids ready to go to the game, and Bernard was helping by washing the last of the breakfast dishes. Little Mary came in with a crayon and saw a wonderful place to write on the wallpaper, but Mrs. Mueller saw her just in time and gently took the crayon out of her hand. "No, no," Mrs. Mueller said, waving a finger in front of Mary's nose. "Time to go to the game, so let's get your brace on.

"No, no, no," Mary said, putting her hands on her hips and pursing her lips out in a pouting gesture. "I don't want to wear it. I don't, I don't, I don't."

"Well, Mary you have to because you will have to be on your feet for most of the rest of the day." Mrs. Mueller picked Mary up and sat her in one of the kitchen chairs and put the brace on and tightened it to a comfortable fit, while Mary fidgeted and wiggled. "There.

How does that feel? Too tight?"

"No, it's okay," Mary said, still pouting. "Can I go outside and play now?"

"Yes, but get your coat, and stay near the house. It's almost time for the game to start and we have to leave soon."

"But, why do I need my coat? I'm not cold."

"I know that you're not cold, now. It's just in case it does get cold, later."

"But the sun is out." She pointed to the window, through which the bright rays of the morning sun shone.

"I know that the sun is out, NOW, Mary, but later--oh, never mind darling. I'll bring your coat. We'll just put it in the van in case you need it."

"I won't need it cause the sun is out."

"Fine," Mrs. Mueller said, giving up on the subject.

Jerry came running into the kitchen then, bounding all over the room like a happy wild deer in a field of clover. "I'm ready. I'm ready. Let's go to the game," he sang as he jumped and skipped all around the room.

"You have your shirt on backwards." Mrs. Mueller pulled it up over his head, got his arms out, then turned it around and slipped it back on.

"Ouch! That hurts my ears," Jerry complained as he wiggled all around.

"Hold still now. We can't go around with your shirt on backwards now, can we? It would look like your head was facing the wrong way."

"Can I get a hot dog at the game?" Jerry asked.

"How can you still be hungry after that big breakfast?"

"I just want a hot dog."

"All right. You can have a hot dog."

"Oh boy. I get a hot dog. I get a hot dog," he said

skipping around in a big circle, then bounding out of the kitchen.

"Anyone want more to eat?" Mrs. Mueller called, so the whole house could hear. There was no answer. "No? All right then, I'll just put the rest of the eggs away and finish up the dishes. Everybody go brush your teeth, then go out and get in the van. Come on kids. Hurry, hurry, hurry. I have to help set up our refreshment stand, so we have to get there a little bit early."

Shooing them all out of the room like a shepherdess with her sheep, she then patted Bernard on the shoulder and bent to speak to him in her best soft, and low whispering voice. Her breath tickled Bernard's ear as she spoke. "Bernard, would you be a dear and dry and finish putting these dishes away for me?"

"Okay."

"We have to be there a little early, so I'll take Mary and Jerry over now. You'll have plenty of time to take your bath, then ride your bike over. All right?"

"Sure."

"Thank you Bernard. You are a dear." She gave him a kiss on the forehead, then said, "See you there."

Bernard looked out the kitchen window and watched them all getting into the van. Mrs. Mueller turned to wave at him one last time, throwing him a pretend kiss by kissing her hand, then making believe that she threw it to him, Bernard made believe he caught it, and then he waved back through the kitchen window, as Mrs. Mueller got in the van and drove away. Bernard finished drying the last flowered dish, then he looked at the big owl clock on the kitchen wall. Seeing that there was plenty of time before the game, he decided to take a long hot bath with his bubbly bath stuff, then he got dressed in his Blue Angels uniform, gathered all his soccer gear together, went down the stairs and out the back door to the garage. It was not until he reached for the doorknob that he noticed the padlock dangling loosely there. Bending closer he saw that the hasp had been cut right in two, and the door was standing slightly ajar. "Oh no!" he said out loud. His heart took a sudden leap. Fearful of what he might find inside, he pulled the door back slowly, then cautiously peeked inside.

"Oh, no," he gasped again. "Superbike has been stolen."

Pulling his watch from his pocket, he looked at the big dial. Just ten minutes left to get to the game. On Superbike he could make it in about four minutes, but without it... Bernard turned and looked up at the hills. They looked very far away now, and the school was clear on the other side of the mountain. He could have made it easily on time with minutes to spare on Superbike but walking would probably take more than an hour. He looked frantically around. The whole town was deserted and as quiet as a cemetery because everyone was at the game, so there wouldn't be anyone around that could give him a ride. What was he to do? It seemed like a completely hopeless situation. For what seemed like a very long time he just stood there with his heart pounding, wondering what to do. Then he put his hand in his pocket and felt the lucky rock that Hal had given him, and then all of a sudden he remembered the Blue Angels chant. "Never give up. Never give up. Never give up." He could almost hear the team singing it in his head. Without even thinking, he moved into action, starting off at a jog toward the distant hills.

CHAPTER SIXTEEN

As soon as the Blue Angels team members began arriving at the field, Coach Bob got them out on the grass kicking the ball, practicing, and warming up. He watched them nervously, looking at his watch often, and pacing up and down the edge of the field calling out instructions to the boys from the sidelines.

Mr. Brown, who had just arrived, walked over and greeted him. "Good morning Bob," he said in his happy morning voice. "How are we doing this morning?"

"Don't ask," Bob said. "We are not doing well, and I'm as nervous as a squirrel that has lost his winter supply of nuts."

"What for?" Mr. Brown said holding onto his usual smile, but with just a hint of worry in his eyes. "It's a beautiful day. The birds are singing, and all the world is right."

"Not exactly," Bob groaned. "It's almost game time

and Bernard Wheel isn't here yet."

"Oh," Mr. Brown laughed. "Nothing to worry about. It's a bad habit Bernard has. He's late to class sometimes, but never by more than a minute or two. I'm sure that he'll be here soon."

"I know that," Bob groaned, "but I warned him that if he was late to this game, I wouldn't let him play in the first quarter."

"Oh, I see," Mr. Brown said. "That's too bad."

"Now, I'm sorry as heck that I said that to him, and worse, that I said it right in front of the whole team, because he's our very best player and I really need him against this Green Hornet team." The coach took a deep breath and let out a big long sigh, "but a promise is a promise, and it's very important that a coach set a good example by always keeping his word."

"You're absolutely right, Bob. It would be awful to lose the game to the other team, but setting a good example by always keeping your word is much more important than winning."

"But sometimes it's real hard to do the right thing, and right now I'm getting really nervous."

The referee named Ralph Pastroni from Devlin Corners, a wiry little man with a big black mustache, came walking over toward Bob and Mr. Brown, calling out,

"Have you got the Blue Angels all ready to play, Bob?"

"We're not quite ready yet, Ralph," Bob answered.

"We were supposed to start at eleven, and it's eleven right now, Bob."

"I know that, Ralph but one of my boys hasn't arrived yet. We need just a few minutes more. Is that okay?" Bob asked.

"Well, I guess that'd be okay," Ralph said, looking

at his watch, "but make it fast, the crowd is getting anxious and Manning and his team are all ready to start."

"I'll make it as fast as I can, Ralph" Bob promised.

"Five minutes, and no more," Ralph said holding up five fingers, then walked back across the field. Then, some of the people in the stands started whistling and yelling and stomping their feet in anticipation of the game starting.

"I'll go look around and see if I can find Bernard," Mr. Brown said walking away.

"I'd appreciate that," Bob called out after him.

Hal came walking through the gate and strolled through the milling crowd of people with Senor Birdy riding on his shoulder, looked around, and found a place to sit in the stands near the fifty yard line. Although he was a stranger in town, nobody seemed to notice him at all. It was almost as if he was invisible.

Coach Bob walked out on the field where the Blue Angels were practicing kicks and controlling the ball, and as he watched, the Old Timer came up behind him, tapped him on the shoulder and yelled as though the coach was hard of hearing.

"Hey Bob," he yelled.

Bob jumped in surprise, then turned and faced the old man. To his amazement, he saw that the old timer was all dressed up in a Blue Angel's uniform and carrying a bucket, some cups and a towel. On the front of the Old Timer's uniform was a big sign in bright red letters saying "Water Boy."

"What are you doing here?" Bob asked.

"Where do you want me to keep the water?" the Old Timer said, ignoring Bob's question, or not hearing it at all.

Bob took a moment to think about it, scratched his head, put his hands on his hips, took a deep breath, then pointing toward the sidelines said, "Put it over behind the Blue Angel's bench." Then Bob saw that the bucket was empty. "But you're going to need water," the coach said, pointing his finger down into the empty bucket.

"What?" the Old Timer said, putting his ear horn in and leaning very close to Bob.

"Water," Bob yelled. "Water, water, WATER!"

"Daughter?" the old timer yelled, smiling broadly. "Oh yes, my daughter is here today. Right over there in the stands with the grandkids."

"Fine," Bob said, giving up on trying to make any contact with the old man.

"Well, I'll go over to the benches now," the Old Timer said, "but I'd better get some water to fill this bucket first."

"Good idea," Bob said as the Old Timer moved off toward the bench.

Jim moved very close to Bob, whispering, "What's he dressed up like that for? This isn't a football game, and nobody has water boys at soccer games."

"I know that," Bob said, "You know that, but HE doesn't know that. Hey, the old man wants to participate, and who am I to discourage him. Anyway, he isn't doing anyone any harm, and someone might actually want some water. And, it might cheer the boys up a little. That would certainly help about now."

"Right," Jim replied. "You're right. I guess it couldn't hurt."

Bob started counting his team again, then looked the boys over to see if Bernard had arrived yet. When he didn't see him he turned his attention to the crowd, then walked over to the soft drink stand where Mrs. Mueller and Little Mary were busily setting up the cups with ice from the cooler. "I've been looking for Bernard," Bob said. "Didn't he come with you?

"No," Mrs Mueller answered, looking shocked. "He was supposed to ride his bike over as soon as he finished his bath. But I haven't seen him. Isn't he with the team?"

"No. I can't find him and we have to start the game pretty soon. Maybe he's around here someplace. I'll ask the boys if anyone knows where he is," Bob said, then disappeared into the crowd.

"Where in the heck is Bernard?" Coach Bob looked at his watch, then all around the field, asking all the boys, but they all just shook their heads. They didn't know.

"Well, he's late a lot," Ernie quipped.

"But he'll be here. He always is," Turtle said.

Coach Bob took off his hat and scratched his head vigorously. "Darn it!" he said out loud, then he clapped his hands together to get the team's attention. "Okay you guys, keep on warming up. And start slow. You know, take your time. Act like you are kinda stiff or something. I need to stall for time. Okay, do it."

Just then Manning came walking up to them with referee Ralph at his side. He looked like a bowl full of jello in his Green Hornet Coach's shirt, his belly hanging out in front over his belt so far that it swayed back and forth as he walked. "Let's get this game underway," he demanded. "My team is all ready and waiting. What's the holdup here? Let's get this show on the road."

Sheriff George and Mr. Brown joined them then. "I don't see why we can't wait just a bit more," Bob said. "My team isn't really warmed up good yet. Just take a look at those boys out there."

Everyone looked and saw that the Blue Angel's were moving around the field so slow that it almost appeared as if they were all in slow motion.

"Come on," Manning yelled angrily. "Cut the

baloney, and let's get to playing this soccer game."

"No, you cut the baloney," Bob yelled back. "That's what you do for a living, Manning. Cut baloney. I don't want any one of my kids to pull a muscle or get hurt, on account of them not being properly warmed up."

"They're gonna get hurt if they play my boys," Manning laughed. "You just want to delay getting your tail whipped, don't you Bob? Well, you can give up if you want to, and we won't even have to embarrass you. You want to forfeit this game?" Manning said, laughing so hard that his belly wiggled like a balloon full of water.

"Wait a minute, you guys," Sheriff George said. We don't want anyone hurt here; this ain't exactly world class soccer, and these kids' games hardly ever start on time. So what's the big deal? Seems like we could spare a few minutes just once, and keep this on a friendly basis."

"Bull," Manning yelled. "It's the State Championship, and rules is rules and if they can't play, then they forfeit. You forfeiting, Bob? Is that what you are doing? Chickening out?"

"Of course not," Bob said, taking a step toward Manning and pushing his face up to his. "We're not chickening out. We're not quitters. We're gonna play, and it might even surprise you to know that I think we can whip your......"

"Not on any Sunday in your lifetime," Manning yelled and raised his fist to hit Coach Bob.

"Hold on, you guys," Mr. Brown said stepping between them. "We came here to watch the kids play soccer, not to watch grown men fighting, so let's just cool it, okay?"

"Okay, then make those sissy Blue Angels play." Manning snorted into Bob's face, and his breath was so foul that Bob had to pull back.

"Wait a minute," George said, jamming his arm

across between them. "No need to get angry, fellas."

A roar went up from the anxious crowd as they watched the pushing and shoving out on the field, and they started to chant and stomp their feet. "Play ball, play ball, play ball." Some were yelling out, "Blue Angels," and others were grunting "Green Hornets," in a low rumbling unison that sounded very ominous and threatening.

"The fans are getting anxious," Ralph said. "They're expecting a game here, and if we don't start soon, we may have a riot on our hands."

"Play or forfeit," Manning growled again.

"We're gonna play," Bob growled back, mocking him.

"Good," Manning snorted. "Then get your stupid team out on the field. We'll show you and your little sissies a thing or two." He shook his fist in Coach Bob's face, then turned and stormed away down the field motioning to all the Green Hornets to follow him to the bench for final instructions.

"Nice guy, that Manning," Mr. Brown said sarcastically.

"Well, what can you expect from a guy who kills animals for a living," Bob snorted. "Anyway, we bought another five minutes by arguing.

Mr. Brown moved in close to Bob as they walked to the sidelines. "You told Bernard that he couldn't play the first quarter if he was late anyway, so we have at least fifteen or twenty minutes to find him before the second quarter. You get the boys ready to play, and I'll drive over to Bernard's house and see if I can find him there. Okay, Bob?"

"Sounds like a good plan," Bob agreed, patted Mr. Brown on the shoulder, then went to call the Blue Angels together to give them their game plan and instructions.

From the stands, the crowd could see that something had been settled down there on the field, and that the coaches were gathering their players together to get their final instructions. Almost everyone stood and applauded long and loud, in anticipation of the start of the game, although the attitude of the fans seemed more hostile than friendly and there was the feeling that this was going to be more of a war than a friendly game between sportsmanlike teams.

"You guys go out there and stomp the living daylights out of those Blue Angels," Manning said. "No mercy for these little punks. Kick their butts into the next county. The're just a bunch of sissies and deserve to be crushed the way you would stomp on a bug, and I want you guys to destroy them. Got that?"

"We'll grind them into the grass," J.D. said.

"Atta boy," Manning said. "Use every dirty trick in the book, but be careful that you don't get caught. We don't want to lose the game on fouls. Hurt them but do it when nobody is looking. You got it?"

"We got it," J.D. said.

Manning patted him on the shoulder. "Good, and it's pizza and ice cream for all of you guys tonight, on me, but only if you win this game."

Don't worry. It's in the bag." J.D. said.

Over at the Blue Angel's bench, Coach Bob addressed his team with a sad and a worried look upon his sunburned face. "Okay you guys, Bernard didn't show up so I have to make some changes in playing positions. Ernie, you move up to play forward, in Bernard's position.

Turtle, you take Ernie's regular position, and Jojo will move up to right forward. Rob, Freddie, John, center, and the rest of you bring up the rear, Tim play right rear guard. Now look, boys, we know that these guys are really tough. They are all bigger than you fellows, and pretty darned strong, so our strategy has to be to play faster and smarter than them, okay guys?"

"That should be easy," Ernie quipped. "None of them is exactly an "A" student."

"Right. But they are VERY big and VERY strong."

Jojo laughed and said, "We'll ambush them and outsmart them the way the Apaches got the Buffalo, who were big and strong, and smelled just like the Green Hornets." And all the rest of the boys laughed and then made Indian whoops, tapping their hands over their mouths. "Wooo, wooo, wooo, wooo, wooo."

Coach Bob slapped Jojo on the back, "You have a good attitude, Jojo," he said. "Just keep on thinking like that and we can win this game."

Then a whistle blew and they all looked up to see the referee in the middle of the field waving for the teams to come out and line up in the center.

"Okay boys, Coach Bob said. "This is it. Come on, but take your sweet time walking out there. Let's lull them into believing that we are all really slow, then, when they least expect it, speed up and sock it to them."

The Blue Angels followed Bob out to the center field line, and the crowd applauded wildly as they all lined up in formation facing the Green Hornets across twenty feet of grass.

"Team captains step forward," Ralph the ref said. Then Ernie and J.D. stepped out to the middle and Ralph asked them to select a side of the big round card, J.D. said, "Black," and Ernie yelled "Okay," then the ref flipped the big card up high. Everyone was looking up, watching it turn slowly in the air. It was then that J.D. used his first dirty trick. Quickly he shot a short but fast kick to Ernie's ankle. Ernie winced in pain and looked around to see if anyone had seen it, but all heads were looking up watching the card slowly turning and nobody had even noticed what J.D. had done. J.D. just smiled at Ernie in his nastiest way, as the card came down and hit the grass, black side up. "I guess we win the kick off," J.D. said grinning a toothy grin.

The crowd was hooting and yelling and stomping as the boys lined up in formation on each side of the field. The ref placed the ball inside the circle for the kick and J.D. smacked it with all his might, sending it soaring through the air toward the Blue Angel's goal. Ernie moved forward, meeting the oncoming ball with his head, "Pang!" it went as it zoomed forward, back toward the oncoming Green Hornets. But before they could intercept it, Jojo ran in and got it. He moved like lightning, weaving in and out of the Green Hornets like a skier on a downhill slalom. Almost to the goal, he got cut off by Spider and Ugly Joe, but Jojo passed the ball to Tim who booted it high up into the air. Spider got to it first, kicking it back along the sideline up the field and back toward the Blue Angel's goal. J.D. was running right by Spider's side, blocking, as Spider got the ball and ran with it. Jojo came on fast, outrunning Spider, catching up to him easily but when he tried to scoop the ball away, Ugly Joe ran up behind him, stepped on the back of his foot causing him to fall, then deliberately ran right over him with his cleated shoes. The referee blew his whistle, called a foul, then gave the ball to the Blue Angels for a throw from the sidelines.

"You are supposed to do it so nobody sees you," J.D. growled at Ugly Joe."

"I hurt his foot real bad," Ugly Joe said smiling proudly.

"That's good," J.D. said. "Just be careful not to be caught next time."

Turtle got the ball and passed it to Ernie who passed it back to Turtle, and in a second or two, the Blue Angels were in Green Hornet territory again. Down near the net, Jojo ran in and the ball was passed to him. Spider and J.D. tried to block him but Jojo booted the ball between their legs, ran around them and took it on down the field so fast that they were left with their mouths hanging open. With one swift kick the ball smashed into the net, and the crowd went wild. The Blue Angels had scored their first goal and it was now Blue Angel's one, Green Hornets, nothing.

J.D. was in shock as he watched the Blue Angels go back to their side to await the next kick.

"You take that little guy out this time," J.D. told Ugly Joe.

"What about the penalty, J.D.?"

"Never mind what Manning said. One penalty won't cost us the game, but he might. He's too fast. Take him out."

On the next play the Blue Angels passed the ball faster and more often, and it made the bigger boys on the Green Hornet team look clumsy and slow, and kind of foolish too. J.D. was getting mad, so, the next time Jojo had the ball, he signalled to Ugly Joe, and Ugly Joe came running right at Jojo from behind, knocking him down by smashing right into him and then deliberately falling on top of Jojo with all his weight.

A hoot and a boo went up from the stands as the whistle blew and the referee came in to stop the action. The ref pulled Ugly Joe up and everyone expected little Jojo to be hurt, but he jumped right up smiling and waved at the crowd as though nothing had happened.

"You can't hurt an Indian with blubber," Jojo said to Ugly Joe, and walked back to his team as the crowd yelled and cheered and applauded.

The ref took the ball and held it high. J.D. came in to jump for it against Turtle, and when they jumped, Turtle knocked the ball toward his team, and J.D. kneed him in the belly. Nobody noticed as J.D. ran after the ball, but Turtle was holding onto his side and grimacing in pain as he limped slowly back into the action.

CHAPTER SEVENTEEN

Far away, on the other side of the mountain, Bernard was jogging up the trail, huffing and puffing all the way until he reached the very top of Blueberry Ridge. From that high hilltop he could see far out over the vast valley below. Sitting on a big rock, breathing hard, and trying to rest, he figured the time and the distance left that he had to travel to the school and realized that before he could get to the game on foot, it would be nearly over. Anyway, he thought, even if he ran all the way, and got there in time for the last quarter, he would probably be too exhausted to play. It all seemed pretty hopeless, but he didn't want to give up. He kept hearing the team chant in his head. Never give up, never give up. Never give up. Looking around he spotted some dead wood, and an idea came to him. Quickly, he gathered the sticks and branches together, stacking them in a pyramid-like pile, then he found two small pieces of flint rock and started knocking them together, making sparks fall onto the dry leaves and dead wood. After a few tries, the leaves began to smoulder. Bernard blew gently on the delicate tinder until a tiny flame burst from one of the leaves. "Wow! Just like in the boy scouts," Bernard said out loud as the fire caught hold, crackled and spread to the wood. "All right!" Bernard said clapping his hands together happily. Then, he quickly took off his shirt, using it to fan the flames until the fire began to roar wildly.

It was the end of the first quarter and the game was getting really rough. Turtle had to help Ernie off the field because the ankle that J.D. had kicked was now swelling, causing him to limp. As they reached the bench, Ernie looked up, and as he did, he noticed something strange. "What is that?" he said, and coach Bob and some of the boys looked where Ernie was pointing.

"Looks like a fire way up there on Blueberry Ridge," Turtle said.

"Smoke signals," Jojo exclaimed.

"Huh?" Bob remarked.

"It's the way us Indians used to send messages long distances way back in the old days."

"I know that," Bob said, "but, are you sure?"

"Of course, I'm sure. See how the puffs come up at different spaces."

"Yes, but what does it say?"

"It's Bernard," Jojo said, reading the smoke message. "He says, 'Bike stolen. Need a ride.'"

"You can't get a car way up there in the forest," Jim said. "You need a horse or something."

"I'll go get him on my trail bike," Jojo said, and before anyone could say another word, Jojo ran to the bike racks, unlocked his machine, mounted and was gone.

The shrill blast of the ref's whistle brought the Blue Angels back to reality and the game at hand. Coach Bob clapped his hands together. "Okay you guys--let's get out there and give em' heck."

Turtle took the ball down the field but Spider was right on his case, bumping him from behind then sticking his foot between Turtle's legs, tripping him. The ball rolled free, then J.D. kicked the ball to Ugly Joe, who took it near the net, then J.D. ran up and smacked it into the net. The crowd roared, some hooting for the Green Hornets, and some shaking their fists in anger, others standing and waving their arms all around in excitement.

"We may have a riot on our hands here," Jim said.

"Not if we can help it," George said, then yelled "Foul!" and ran over to talk to the ref.

This time a penalty was assessed, the point was taken away, and the Angels got the ball. But J.D. ran in again, stole it away, elbowed Freddy in the ribs then ran with the ball, and scored a point. This time it was allowed and the score was now one to one.

"Gee whiz," Turtle was puffing hard, out of breath as he got pulled back up to his feet by his team. "These guys are really playing dirty!"

"I know," Ernie said. "It's a bummer, but we have to keep on fighting and doing our best, and never, never give up, just like the coach told us."

"I know," Jim agreed, looking off toward the Purple Mountains. "But we are losing our best players, and I sure do wish that Bernard and JoJo were here."

CHAPTER EIGHTEEN

Bernard was waiting by the smoldering ashes of the dying campfire when Jojo came pedaling up the hill.

"How's the game going?" was the first thing that Bernard asked.

"We got one goal in the first quarter," Jojo said.

"How about the Green Hornets?"

"So far they haven't scored. It's one to nothing."

"Great," Bernard said. Then he pointed down at the loose dirt in the path near his fire. "Look over here, Jojo. See that tire track there in the soft dirt?"

The young Indian put his kickstand down, then came to look closely where Bernard was pointing. "Yeah?"

"It's the print of my bike tire, and I never ever rode on this part of this trail in my life. That means that whoever stole my bike, rode it right past this place."

"Who stole your bike?"

"Well, I don't know for sure, Jojo. It was gone

when I went out to get it to come to the game today, but I can guess that it was someone that didn't want me to play."

"You think J.D., or someone in his gang stole it?"

"Maybe, but I don't want to accuse anyone until I know for sure."

"Yeah, I guess that's fair. Well, hop on my bike, and I'll take you back to the game. We can use your help. Those guys are playing pretty dirty."

"But, you said that we were ahead, one to nothing. So I want to follow these tracks and see if I can get my bike back before whoever stole it gets too far away, and strips it."

"But, how can you tell that those tracks are your bike tire?"

"See that little line across the tread right there?" Bernard pointed at the marks in the wet dust of the road.

"Looks like a little cut," Jojo said.

"Right. Well, that's where I ran over a piece of glass and cut the tire about a week ago. It didn't hurt my tire much, but it makes it a very positive identifying mark."

"I see," JoJo said. "And look, the tracks lead down the ridge toward Farmer's Flats."

Bernard shaded his eyes from the sun and peered out over the green valley below where a few old farm houses and barns could be seen far away in the distance. "Right." he said. "I think we should follow those tracks while they are fresh. Maybe we can find my bike."

"Okay, but, what about the game?" Jojo started to say, but Bernard jumped on his handlebars and pointed ahead. "We have time to get to the game, so let's go this way and see if we can find my bike first."

"Okay," Jojo said pushing off, and together they started down the slope toward the valley far below.

There was an old two lane paved road at the bottom of the trail. They stopped to look. Jojo got off and knelt beside the pavement.

"Look here, Bernard. You can see the dirt on the road here where the bikes turned. There were five of them, it looks like, maybe four, and yours. And, they all went that way toward those old farm houses." Jojo pointed down the road. Then, jumping back on his bike, and with Bernard sitting on the handlebars, he pedalled down the old road, looking for more signs of tire marks.

Suddenly Jojo slammed on the brakes, and Bernard had to hold on tight to keep from falling off. Bernard held the bike up as Jojo knelt and examined the shoulder of the road. "Hey," he cried out excitedly, "look over here."

Bernard put the kickstand down and came over to take a closer look. "See," Jojo said pointing at the dirt. "They turned off here. Looks like they cut across this grass and up to those trees."

Up ahead was an old barn that looked as if it had been abandoned for a good many years, and the boys followed the bike tracks right up to the door. "Look at this." Bernard held the lock on the door in his hand for Jojo to see. "There's a brand new lock on this dilapidated old barn door."

"Seems kinda funny, huh?"

"Makes you wonder what they might be hiding in there."

"Maybe we can find a hole or something that we can see through."

The boys started looking around until they found a loose board that they were able to pry back far enough to look inside. "Hey," Bernard cried out in joy. "Superbike is in there."

"Is it okay?"

"It looks okay to me. I guess they didn't have time to strip it, or anything."

"Maybe we'd better go call the Sheriff," Jojo said.

"No, we can't do that. He's at the game."

"Oh, right. I forgot."

"Help me get this board off. I'm going to get my bike." Bernard found a tree limb and pried a high board off. It was just enough so that he could slip through and drop to the floor of the barn inside.

"I can't get through that hole," Jojo complained. "I'm too big."

"You just stay out there and keep your eyes open," Bernard said, "just in case somebody comes along."

"What will I do if those crooks come back?"

"Just whistle or something. I don't know. Hide."

"Looks all clear, so far, Bernard."

"Hey, it looks like my bike is okay," Bernard called out.

"We'd better get out of here quick. I see a car coming down the road. It might be the crooks."

Jojo ran behind a tree and slid down in the tall grass behind it, while Bernard peeked out through a crack in the barn doors, ready to run and hide, but the car just passed on the road, disappearing around a bend down the way.

"It's okay," Jojo said, coming back to the barn.

"I'm going to get my bike out of here," Bernard said, "before someone comes back and gets it."

"Don't you think we should get back to the game and let the Sheriff handle this?" Jojo asked. But Bernard just said, "Nope, I'm going to get Superbike."

He went around trying all the doors on the inside but they all had padlocks on them and he couldn't get any of them open. Then he found a window that had a sliding board holding it in place. He pushed the locking plank out, then shoved the big shutter open. The sunlight streamed into the barn. He waved to Jojo.

"I got the window open."

"But it's too high to get your bike out, Bernard. We'd better just go and get some help."

"I've got an idea," Bernard said, dragging a big wooden plank over to the window. He leaned one side up on the window sill with the other side on the floor. "Stand back Jojo," he called out. "I'm coming through."

Then Bernard took Superbike to the very back of the barn, getting a good run to the bottom of the plank. Zap, his front tire hit the wooden ramp and up he went to the window, then out into the air, soaring out over Jojo's head like a big bird.

"Wow," Jojo exclaimed as he saw Bernard land in the road, do a wheelie, then skid to a stop. Bernard turned back and waved at Jojo. "Come on," he called out. "Get your Indian legs in motion and let's get our bodies to that game before it's over."

Riding like the wind, Jojo and Bernard traversed the road and took the long downhill path toward the soccer game.

CHAPTER NINETEEN

The roar of the crowd rose like a cannon shot into the still warm air, frightening the birds from the nearby trees as Turtle stole the ball from Spider Kramer and kicked it down the field toward Ernie. Every eye followed that ball as Ernie passed it to Rob. Rob ran with it, then passed it back to Ernie who took off running. Spider took that opportunity to run up behind Turtle and give him a vicious kick in the ankle. Nobody noticed as Spider ran away with the ball, leaving Turtle limping to the sidelines in pain.

Spider was surrounded by the Blue Angels so he kicked the ball into the air toward J.D. Rob saw the ball coming toward J.D., ran in, and, jumping up, he took the ball on his forehead. "Pong," it went, and the ball sailed away and the Blue Angels took it up the field again. Rob turned and threw a smile at J.D. and J.D. smiled back, then stepped forward and kneed Rob in the groin. Little

Mary saw it and ran out onto the field screaming, "Cheater, cheater, cheater," and started hitting J.D. with both her little fists. The referee blew his whistle then, and stopped the game. People stood up in the stands and yelled, and yelled, and then everything stopped as Sheriff George and Deputy Jim ran over and pulled Little Mary away just as J.D. raised his arm to hit her.

"What happened here?" the Sheriff asked.

"She attacked me just cause her team is losing," J.D. lied.

"He's cheating, cheating, cheating," Mary screamed as the Sheriff and Jim carried her back to the sidelines kicking and screaming and Mrs. Mueller took hold of her.

"Calm down," Mrs. Mueller said. "Let the Sheriff handle this."

As all this commotion was going on, Bernard and Jojo came riding in at full speed, sliding their bikes to a stop right at the team's bench. Everyone stopped fighting, and Coach Bob raised his arm, yelling, "time out." Then he and Little Mary, and Mrs. Mueller, and all the Blue Angels surrounded Bernard and Jojo.

"What happened to you?" coach Bob asked Bernard.

"My bike was stolen, but I got it back, and I'm here now. Can I play, coach?"

"Yeah. Me too," Jojo put in. "I want to play too." Rob came limping off the field then, dropping down heavily on the bench. "He can take my place coach," Rob cried out. "I think my ankle might be broken."

"Someone get the doctor to look at that ankle," Bob cried out, then turning to Bernard and Jojo he said, "I can put you both in as substitutes." The whole Blue Angel's team let out a big "Whoopee," they were so happy.

Manning pushed closer to them saying, "Wait a minute here. You can't just put these guys in the game in the middle. This ain't no popularity contest, you know."

"The heck I can't," Bob yelled at him, getting in Manning's face.

"You can not." Manning yelled back.

"He can too," Referee Ralph declared. "He can substitute any other player for any injured player. That's the rules, and besides that, Manning, I saw the kick that Spider gave this boy and I'm calling another foul on your team."

"What? A foul?" Manning objected. "I didn't see any foul. There was no foul."

"I saw it too," Little Mary screamed. "He kicked Rob in the ankle, and that's no fair. No fair, no fair, no fair."

"And I saw it too," Deputy Jim, put in.

"And so did I," Sheriff George said. "I saw the kick."

The ball was tossed to referee Ralph then and he held it high over his head, announcing to the stands, "The foul stays." All the people there stood up and yelled so loud that it was like a clap of thunder, sending a shock wave through the air.

"Spider is out of the game for the duration," the ref continued, "and Bernard Wheel and Jojo are in as substitutes, and the Blue Angels get a free goal kick." So saying, ref Ralph walked out on the field and placed the ball on the line in front of the Green Hornets goal net. The crowd started to settle down then, taking their seats slowly and getting real quiet.

Over on the sidelines, behind the Green Hornets bench, Manning grabbed Spider's shoulder and secretly pushed a small bottle of pills into his hand. "This guy Bernard is too good and too tough," Manning whispered into Spider's ear. "Here, take these pills and sneak over there and dump them into the Blue Angel's water bucket when nobody is looking."

Spider nodded that he understood, and slipped the bottle of pills under his shirt, then walked casually toward the Old Timer, who was watching the game at the sidelines nearby.

Out on the field the teams took their positions, and Bernard got into place to make the kick. By the time he was ready, there was a dead silence out there on the field with only the sound of the wind blowing softly through the trees, and an occasional bird chirping far away.

Bernard stepped back, then suddenly moved forward and smashed the ball perfectly on the toe of his soccer shoe. "Whack! it went, and like a shot out of a cannon, it went straight through the Green Hornet line so fast that they could barely see it, much less stop it, and it hit the back of the net so hard that it stretched the net out. The crowd jumped up and gigantic roar went up that rattled the windows a hundred yards away in the school building. In all the excitement, nobody noticed Spider empty the bottle of pills into the Blue Angel's water bucket.

Bernard was congratulated by his team, who slapped his hand and patted him on the back, and for the first time since he got back, he looked up at the scoreboard and the smile slowly left his face. As Mr. Cooper put the new numbers up, Bernard saw that the score was now Green Hornets four, Blue Angels two, and there were only four minutes left to play in the game.

Ralph, the ref said. "Okay, teams take your sides for the kick off, and let's play soccer."

"We're running out of time," Turtle said as the teams walked to their positions.

Bernard walked close to Ernie, Turtle and Jojo, and said, "We have to take a big risk now. Are you guys ready?"

They all signaled that they were, and Bernard said,

"Okay guys, you know what to do."

J.D. kicked the ball with a mighty smack, so that it sailed right over Bernard's head and landed near the Blue Angel's goal. Then the Green Hornet team came charging down the field like a herd of crazy buffalo. Jojo got the ball, and kicked it to Ernie who slipped through the big boys and made it up the field a few yards. Cornered by J.D. and Ugly Joe, he passed the ball right through J.D.'s legs to Turtle who passed it back to Jojo. The little Indian boy moved fast, zig zagging among the bigger Green Hornets, and got the ball over the half way line, before he passed it to Bernard. Bernard kicked the ball up in the air and Ernie caught it on his forehead, slamming it back to Bernard, who passed it back to Jojo. In this way the Blue Angel's got the ball up in Green Hornet territory. Then, in one quick move, Turtle moved near the net and bent, holding his knees, Jojo passed the ball to Bernard, and Bernard gave it a mighty kick. "Whacko! Pong!" went the ball as it left Bernard's shoe, hit Turtle's behind, and glanced right into the net. The crowd went crazy, and smiles were all over the Blue Angel's faces as they shook hands and walked up the field to take their positions to receive the next kickoff, while the Green Hornets stood there dumbfounded.

Coach Bob ran out on the field and talked to the boys.

"That was a great play," he told them, "but I don't think you can get away with it twice. We need one more point to tie them and get into overtime. This time we stick to the practiced moves, okay? Do number six, okay guys?" The boys all nodded, yes, and Coach Bob said, "Go get em' boys."

"I feel kind of dizzy," Ernie said as they took their places to receive the kick.

"Me too," Jojo agree. "I shouldn't have drunk that

water. Did you drink anything, Bernard?"

"Naw, I wasn't thirsty. "Hey, you think they put something in the water?"

"Seems like those who drank are feeling bad and the boys that didn't feel okay."

"Maybe we should ask for some substitutes for Jojo and Ernie," Turtle said.

Bernard thought of calling time out for a second. "Naw," he said. "They're our best players. We need them. Fight it guys. Come on. We can beat these guys if we really try."

The kick came flying right at Bernard and he caught it on his belly, knocking the ball back up the field, then chasing after it, but the Green Hornets got the ball and started up the field. Jojo got the ball, but the Green Hornets got it back as Jojo started to stagger like a drunken sailor. Soon the Hornets were at the Blue Angel's goal and try as they did, they just could not get the ball away from the Green Hornets. Time after time they stopped them from getting a goal, but they just could not get the ball back, or move the play up the field to the other side. Jojo and Ernie tried their best, but they were just staggering around like drunks on the field and game time was running out, so when Turtle finally got the ball, he passed it to Bernard and Bernard ran with it, but he was surrounded by Green Hornets and didn't know what to do. Suddenly he looked up at the stands, and there he saw in a flash, Hal sitting there with Senor Birdy on his shoulder, smiling at him. Bernard remembered the lucky rock that Hal had given him and quickly he touched the pocket that it was in, feeling it's roundness there under the material. Looking up at the clock he realized that he had only seconds left in the game, but a sudden inspiration came to him, and as he touched the rock, he heard a little voice in his head telling him what to do.

Bernard moved quickly to a position where he could see the other goal so very far away, but the voice in his head said, "You can do it."

Suddenly J.D. was right in front of him, blocking his path. Bernard ran right at him, kicking the ball with all his might, right between J.D.'s legs. Whaaak! it went with a mighty sound. Upward the ball sailed, high into the clear blue Arizona sky. Then the stands and all the players just stopped where they were, like frozen statues, and watched as the ball soared across the sky, looping up and over the field. There was no one there to stop it as it sailed the full seventy-five yards, landing perfectly in the net, just as the final whistle blew.

"We go into overtime with the score tied at four to four." referee Ralph called out.

Both teams walked toward the sidelines, with Ernie and Jojo both being helped off the field by their team mates. The Doctor treating Freddie's ankle looked up at the drunken boys, then went to check them out. "These boys have been drugged," he said, then he looked at the water bucket, putting his hand in the water and smelling it. "This is Helcetimen," he said, "the same drug that I prescribed for Mr. Manning just the other day," the doctor said. Then he picked up an empty bottle that was lying on the grass near the bucket. "And here is the bottle. It even has Manning's name on it."

Manning shot a look at Spider, who tried to hide behind J.D.

"We'll have to investigate this," ref Ralph said. "But right now it looks like the Green Hornets are going to have to forfeit because of unnecessary roughness, too many fouls, and cheating."

"Too much roughness?" J.D. yelled. "I'll show you some roughness," and he ran forward and took a swing at ref Ralph, but he missed and his gang grabbed him and pulled him back.

"Well, if there wasn't cause enough before," the ref said, "there certainly is now. Trying to hit a referee is definitely cause for forfeiture. The winners of this game are the Blue Angels."

There was a big noise from the crowd, some people cheering and some people really mad that the Green Hornets had lost, and they all stood up and started out of their seats at once, like a herd of cattle stampeding, so that the whole place was in a terrible turmoil.

"Let's all try to stay calm here," the Sheriff shouted, but it was too late. The place was completely out of control.

CHAPTER TWENTY

The Sheriff was standing on the sidelines behind the Blue Angel's bench, watching closely, worried that some fights might break out, when Deputy Jim came up behind him and tapped him on the shoulder. "Sheriff," he said, "I have to tell you something important."

"What, Jim?" the Sheriff said, keeping his eye on the crowd.

"I was just out at the bike racks, and you know that bike that kid J.D. is riding?"

"Yeah, what about it?'

"Well, it has a cowhide bike seat on it."

"So? That don't mean much. Lots of bikes have cowhide seats."

"Yeah, but this has a brand on it, and there's a piece out of his Shomoyo brake handle."

The Sheriff turned with interest to Jim then. "No kidding? Well, that just might mean something. Show it to me," he said, and followed Jim out toward the parking lot.

Nearby, Spider was watching the Sheriff and the Deputy make their way toward the parking lot and when they stopped by the bike racks and started looking over the bicycles. Spider gave J.D. a poke. "Hey, look, J.D." he said.

J.D. looked and saw the Sheriff and Jim examining the bikes. "Looks like they have us nailed," J.D. said.

"And if they don't get us, Manning will," Spider said. "He lost a lot of money betting on this game, and here he comes."

J.D. and the boys looked to see Manning, red faced and angry, walking toward them.

"Come on guys," J.D. said. He motioned, then led the gang through the crowd and around to the backside of the refreshment stands. They hid there and watched until the Sheriff and Jim had examined the bikes, then started walking back toward the field, looking for them.

"We'll wait a minute, then split," J.D. told the boys, then something caught his eye. Nearby, at the back of Mrs. Mueller's booth, they could see her counting the cash she had made that day, and putting it into a little bag with a pull string on it. She gave the bag to Little Mary to hold, as she closed up and they came out of the stand and walked toward the van.

J.D. ran up and grabbed the bag, knocking little Mary to the ground, then the boys made a bee line for their bikes and took off toward the hills. Little Mary started screaming, "Robbers, robbers, robbers!"

Bernard looked up in time to see J.D., Spider, Ugly Joe and Wimp burn rubber out of the parking lot and head for the hills. He and his friends took off for the parking lot and their bikes to give chase.

Bernard, Turtle, Ernie, Jojo, and Tim rode away with the Sheriff and Deputy Jim right behind in the old woody. Jim and the Sheriff raced after the boys, the old Ford kicking up a cloud of dust as they left the pavement and headed over the fields toward the hills.

"Can you see them?" Sheriff George asked in a quavering voice as the Ford wagon bumped and shuddered over the rough dirt road.

"They disappeared up the hill and into the trees," Jim said hanging on with all his might. Then, George put on the brakes and skidded to a stop, with the cloud of dust following them closing in so that they couldn't see a thing until it cleared. The Sheriff peered through the dirty windshield. "The Randolph ranch is right over there," he said. "We'll borrow a couple of horses from them." Then he spun the car around and drove down the road toward the Randolph Ranch.

CHAPTER TWENTY ONE

J.D stopped at the top of Eagle's Nest Ridge and looked back. "You see anything?" he asked. Ugly Joe, who was at the very back of the pack, had some spyglasses and looked back through the tall trees and down the hill. "It's Bernard and the other guys," he said. "I see them."

"How many are there?"

"Looks like about ten."

"Where?" J.D. asked in disgust.

"Down there near the big rocks, coming fast." Ugly Joe pointed. J.D took the glasses from him and peered down the hill. "Dang it!" he exclaimed. "Well, we have a good ten minutes head start on them. Let's ride over to the caves," J.D. said. "We can hide in there until it gets dark." Then he waved the gang on, and sped off with the gang following close behind.

Bernard pulled up at Bubbling Brook and looked in all directions, then scratched his head. It looked like J.D and his gang had just disappeared. "Where in the heck did they go?" he muttered out loud to himself.

Jojo parked his bike and stooped, looking closely at the ground, moving slowly in a wide circle up in front of the other boys. "Broken twig here," he called out, "and some rocks turned over. They went that way up the hill to the top."

"How can you tell that?" Ernie asked.

"Easy as pie for an Indian," Jojo smirked. "These rocks would be dry from the sun on the top side, and wet underneath, if they hadn't been turned over, but they are wet and dark on the top sides, which means that they were turned over recently."

Turtle pushed his bike near where Jojo sat and took a long careful look at the rocks. "How do you know that? Maybe some hiker walked this way and took a drink from his canteen, and spilled some water?"

"No way," Jojo said. "If you look real close at this rock, you will see that the underside is stained from being wet a long time, and right there, a tiny part of a tire imprint on the wet side."

"I think Jojo is right. They headed in that direction all right, but just to make sure we don't lose them, we'd better split up. Jojo and I will go straight ahead. Ernie and Tim go out to the left, and Turtle and Freddie far to the right. We'll all meet at the top of that high ridge. One of us might see something that way. If you do, yell out. Come on guys, let's get after them before they get away."

At Bernard's signal they all mounted their bikes and rode off looking for J.D. and the Dirty Skunk Gang.

Meanwhile, back at the Randolph ranch, Sheriff George and Deputy Jim saddled up a couple of horses and headed out across the fields toward Blueberry Ridge on the mountain trail.

Galloping across the fields, they made good time,

but then had to slow as they negotiated up the narrow path through the trees and the rocks toward the path that ran along Saguaro Cactus Ravine. "I hope we can find them before Bernard and the boys do," the Sheriff said. "If Bernard catches up to them, there could be a fight and somebody could get hurt."

"Gee, this is just like being a real cowboy in the old wild west," Jim commented.

"Yeah," George said, "except in the movies they always did it in the daytime."

Jim looked up at the sky. It was beginning to turn a faint pink with tiny red streaks cutting through it. "Oh, my gosh," Jim said. "I never thought about that. It's getting dark out here."

"Let's just hope that the moon will come out," George said. "We wouldn't want to get stuck out here on horseback on a real dark night. It could be dangerous."

"You mean because of mountain lions and bears and stuff?"

"No. I mean these horses can't see in the dark any better than we can, and they might just step right off a cliff, or stumble in a hole, or step on a rock and throw us off on our heads."

"Golly, I never thought about that."

"Horses are pretty dumb animals, you know. They think we know what we are doing, so they just keep on going, thinking we can guide them. I had an old friend that tried to ride a horse home on a dark night and he fell asleep while riding, and the danged horse walked him right out onto the highway smack dab in front of an eighteen wheeler coming down the road at seventy miles per hour."

"Golly, well what happened?"

Suddenly the Sheriff saw something ahead. "Look," he pointed, "something way up on the ridge ahead. Come on Jim," he said whipping nis horse and galloping away with Jim following close behind.

A few minutes later the sun was setting behind the Purple Mountains and the sky looked like it was on fire. Darkness was closing in fast and the air was filled with the smell of the trees and there was a hum in the air as the gnats came swarming out of the trees and bushes through the shadows. Soon the crickets would sing their songs as night descended upon the empty spaces in the mountains of Arizona.

"I'm gonna get that Bernard if it's the last thing I ever do," J.D. said as he huddled against the damp wall of the cave and shivered.

"What are we going to do now?" Spider said. "I'm getting hungry, and it's cold in here."

"Let's get some wood and light a fire." Wimp said.

J.D. reached out and grabbed his arm as he started to get up. "You ain't going nowhere. No fire," he snarled. "Someone will see the smoke or the light and they'll have us all in jail before morning."

"It'd be warm, and they'd feed us, at least," Joe said.

"You shut up," J.D. said. "If they get you, they get us all and I'm not going to jail."

"So, what are we going to do?" Spider asked.

"As soon as it's safe, we'll make it back to the hideout. I've got some money stashed there, then we can go over to California and just hang out on the beach."

Spider perked up. "We could surf and all that stuff?"

"Right," J.D. said. "Its warm there and we can just live on the beach."

"So what will we do for money?" Ugly Joe asked.

"You just leave that to me, dummy. I'll find us another gig. Didn't I take care of all you guys here?"

"Yeah J.D., but they don't have cows to steal on the beach." Wimp said.

"So, we'll rob stuff out of cars, snatch purses, and stuff like that. You just leave it to me. I'll figure it out."

"Stealing cars would be fun," Spider said "but I don't know how to drive yet."

"Shut up Spider. Listen, Joe, you go out and look around. See if anyone is around. It's dark now, so we might be able to ride on out of here."

Joe went out, and was back after a few minutes. "I looked all over and didn't see anybody," he said.

"Okay," J.D. said. "Let's sneak on down the mountain, and be quiet about it."

The crickets were buzzing loudly, and the night birds were singing as the gang mounted their bikes and rode as quietly as they could down the mountain trail, and in a little while they were on the other side and riding down the road to the old barn that they called their hideout.

Once they arrived, they went inside, parked their bikes and lit a couple of lanterns. J.D. went right to a big hay bin and fumbled around until he found a metal box. He opened it and stuffed the cash into his jacket, then pulled a gun and stuck it under his belt. Spider's eyes popped out when he saw the pistol.

"Gee, J.D., where'd you get that gun?"

"I stole it from my old man's dresser. Where'd you think I got it stupid?'

"What do you need a gun for?" Spider asked.

"Maybe I'll use it on you," J.D. said, pointing the gun at Spider's head and cocking the hammer back. "If you ask too many questions."

"I'll be quiet as a mouse," Spider said, and J.D. put

the gun back in his belt. "Okay, guys, lets mount up and head for the border."

They all went for their bikes but then a voice came down from the hay loft above, saying, "I don't think you should go."

They all looked up and saw Jojo standing there. Surprised, J.D. faced him and yelled up. "What are you doing up there?"

"I'm making a citizen's arrest," Jojo said. "You guys all have to stay here until the police come."

"Oh yeah," J.D. said. "And who is going to make us?"

"We are," came a chorus of voices from all around them and as J.D. and his gang looked, Ernie stood up from behind a bale of hay, Turtle and Tim came out from behind a stack of boards, Rob and Freddie came in through a window, and Bernard stepped into the light from a dark corner of the barn. "We have you outnumbered and surrounded," Bernard said, "so you better turn over the cash that you stole from the soccer game."

J.D. was stunned for a moment, then he pulled the silver gun from beneath his jacket and aimed it up at Jojo. "We ain't outnumbered as long as I have this," he sneered. "Everybody get your hands up, and you, Jojo, get down here where I can see you."

The Blue Angels all looked for instructions to Bernard who slowly put his hands up. They all followed suit, then Jojo grabbed a rope and swung down from the hayloft; aiming right for J.D., he smashed into him and the gun went skidding across the floor. Bernard dove to the floor and grabbed it but the Dirty Skunks were upon him and wrestled it away from him.

"Bring him here," J.D. ordered, and the gang brought Jojo and Bernard over to him and gave the gun back to J.D.

"I've been wanting to teach you a lesson for a long time Bernard, and now I'm gonna make you sorry you ever messed with me."

He took the pistol and cocked it then, extending his arm, he pointed it right at Bernard's head.

"Wait, J.D." Spider yelled.

J.D. held the gun steady, but turned his eyes toward Spider. "What, Spider," he hissed.

"Cattle rustling and stealing bikes is okay, J.D., but I don't think we need to shoot anyone."

"You know that in this State, rustling is a capital offense?" J.D. said.

"I didn't know that," Spider said.

"So, it's the same punishment as for murder. We got nothing to lose, and I don't want to leave any witnesses."

"Don't worry, Spider," Bernard said calmly. He can't shoot anybody with that gun, anyway."

"What makes you say that?" J.D. asked, puzzled.

"Because, I unloaded it while I had it. That's why."

"You didn't have time, and I would've see you do it."

"No you wouldn't J.D., because the hand is quicker than the eye."

"It is not."

"Sure it is. Look for yourself."

"J.D. pulled the gun away from Bernard's head and looked at it to see if it was loaded. Then in a flash of a second, so fast that his hand was only a blur, Bernard reached out and just snatched the gun away from J.D. It was such a quick movement and such a surprise to J.D. that he just stood there with his mouth hanging open like some kind of carnival clown. "See," Bernard said, "I told you that the hand was quicker than the eye."

Then the Blue Angels all jumped on the Dirty Skunks and in a matter of minutes had them all tied up.

Outside the sound of hoofbeats were heard and just as the boys had finished tying up the bad kids, Sheriff George and Deputy Jim came riding up, dismounted, and entered the barn with guns drawn.

"Well," George said. "I see that you boys have been doing my work for me. Thanks a lot. Jim, get on the walkie talkie and call a car to take these boys away."

"Yes sir."

Jojo brought J.D.'s gun over to the Sheriff. "They had this gun, Sheriff," he said.

"Careful with that," George said. "It might go off."

"No danger of that, Sheriff," Turtle said. "Bernard unloaded it."

"That's right," Jojo said, aiming the gun up at the ceiling and squeezing the trigger. "No," Bernard tried to say, but it was too late. There was a powerful "BANG!" as the gun went off so loud that all the boys had to cover their ears, and a big hole was blown in the roof of the barn, with hay and dirt and dust filtering down upon them.

"Give it to me," the Sheriff said.

"I thought you said you unloaded it," Jojo asked Bernard.

"I said that," Bernard said, "but I was only bluffing." Then there was a call from Deputy Jim, from behind. "I think you should look over here, Sheriff," he said, and George walked over to where Jim stood.

"Looks like a lot of stolen bikes," Jim said, "and parts of other stolen bikes."

"And they have cowhide seats," the Sheriff mused. "Seems like we have more than one crime solved here tonight and we have Bernard Wheel and the Blue Angels to thank for cracking this case wide open."

"But there's one thing more that you should see, Sheriff," Jim said sadly pointing to a bike off to one side parked in the shadows. The Sheriff peered into the dark corner, then moved slowly toward it to get a better look. When he was next to the bike he looked down to see the pure white fur covering the bike seat. It glowed in the dim light with a shininess that was unmistakable. "Oh, my God," the Sheriff blurted out. "It's Snowball."

CHAPTER TWENTY TWO

Hal was sitting on a big rock overlooking the lake whittling on a stick and whistling a tune when Bernard came riding down the mountain trail.

"Bernard's coming," Senor Birdy chirped into Hal's ear.

"I see him," Hal replied.

Bernard parked his bike and climbed up on the rock beside Hal.

"Hello, Bernard," Senor Birdy chirped.

"Hi," Bernard said. "I've been looking all over for you, Hal. I couldn't even find the campsite."

"I like to move around at lot. It keeps a little adventure in my life."

"A lot of stuff has happened that I wanted to tell you about."

"Really? What kind of stuff?"

"Well, the Sheriff caught the rustlers, and we won

our soccer game, and I have to thank you for that. I did what you told me, and I kicked this ball, trying to hold it up with my mind, and it went right in the goal."

"It was a great shot, Bernard. I saw it."

"I thought I saw you at the game, but I wasn't sure."

"Yep. I was there and I saw it all, and you and your team were outstanding."

"But the Dirty Skunks stole all the money from the game and we had to chase them to get it back."

"I know. I know all about it."

"How did you know that?"

Hal pulled a paper out of his pocket and laid it on the rock between them. "It's all in the paper, here."

"Oh, of course, but you didn't hear about Little Mary, cause she just got home from the hospital today. They fixed her foot, and in a few weeks she will be out of the cast, and they say she'll walk just as good as anybody in the world when it heals up."

"That is really good news, Bernard, and you should be very proud of yourself for that."

"Me? I didn't do anything. The doctors fixed it."

"You did a lot. You cared enough about her to face danger and get that money back. It was your capacity to love that made it all possible, Bernard, and improving your capacity to love, and taking action when duty calls you, is what life is all about."

"It is? I don't think that I understand."

Hal reached over and put his arm around Bernard and hugged him. "You don't have to understand it in your consciousness to be a good person, Bernard. Some people just are, without even knowing or thinking about it."

"You should meet Little Mary some time, Hal. I think she would like you just like I do."

"Maybe the next time I'm in this part of the world," Hal said.

"You're not going, are you? We were just getting to know each other."

"I know, and I really do enjoy talking to you Bernard, but my stay here is over now, and it's time to move on, but I want to ask a favor of vou before I go."

"What favor, Hal?"

"Well, you see, where I'm going, I need to travel light, and I was wondering if I could leave Senor Birdy with you, until I get back."

"Well, gee, I'd really like that, but I'd have to ask Mrs. Mueller first."

"Awwwk, Mrs. Mueller. Nice lady."

"Well, you just take Senor Birdy home with you. Let her meet him, and I know it will be all right."

"But what if she says no."

"She won't if you ask her nicely. Say it's a favor for a friend."

"But she might say no."

"Well, if she does, you just let Senor Birdy fly back to me. He always knows how to find me, but I know she will say, 'Yes.' You see, Bernard, when you think positive, you send positive brain waves into the universe, and they bring back positive things. Remember jumping the bike, and kicking that ball? Everything is possible, when you believe."

"Okay, Hal. I'll ask."

So, with Senor Birdy on his shoulder, Bernard rode back through the forest to Mrs. Mueller's house. It was a beautiful and happy day, although Bernard was sad at the same time that Hal was going away.

Deputy Jim pulled the Ford wagon up in front of the Sheriff's office and went inside. Sheriff George was reading the paper, but put it down and said, "Howdy, Jim."

"Morning Sheriff."

"The juvenile officers came and took the boys over to the city jail so they are gone. So you don't have any prisoners to worry about today."

"Well, gee, that's good. What do you think they'll do to them?"

"Well, I guess they'll have to go to trial, since the crimes were felonies and all. No telling what a jury will do. Probably give them some time in reform school along with some counseling to see if they can straighten those boys out."

"I surely hope they'll do that. I truly hate to see any young boys get started down that wrong road on the way to a life of crime."

"Me too, but what can you do? They knew what they were doing and they did it anyway, so now there's a price to be paid. It's too bad, but that's just the way it is. You only get one chance in life, and you'd best not blow it."

"I reckon. But it sure is sad."

"And they arrested Manning for buying stolen beef, and took him to jail up in Flagstaff. He says that it was the boys that put him up to it, but I kinda think it was the other way around. Well, I'm sorta tired, so I guess I'll just get my hat and mosey on home."

"Anything special you want me to do tonight, Sheriff?"

"Nope, the whole town is quiet as a rabbit hiding from a hungry eagle at feeding time. Just the way we like it, so I guess you can make your usual rounds, and just take her easy."

"Say, there is something I wanted to ask you before you go, Sheriff. I wanted to ask you before, but we got kinda busy, and then I didn't want to bother you lately, because of your cat."

"Did I tell you, I got another cat. Another white kitten. I call her Snowball the second. But, that's another story. What is it you wanted to ask me, Jim?"

"Well sir, it's about that friend of yours that fell asleep on the horse. You were telling me he rode right out in front of a semi-truck, and then you never did tell me what ever happened."

"Oh, sure," the Sheriff said, and just as he was about to speak, the phone rang. "Dang," he said, picking it up. A look of shock came over his face, and he blurted out, "Be right there honey," and hung up the phone.

"That was the Mrs., Jim. She said there is a mountain lion in our back yard, so we'd better get right over there. Come on, I'll tell you about what happened to old Jaspers and his horse and that semi-truck on the way over." Then the Sheriff and Jim went out the door, climbed into the old Ford woody and drove away quickly.

That evening, Turtle, Jojo and Ernie all came over and yelled at Bernard, who was out in the back yard, polishing Superbike.

"Come on, Bernard," Jojo yelled. "We're riding up to the top of the Mosquito Bite Trail. You want to come along?

Turtle held up a bag full of fluffy white balls. "I'm bringing some marshmallows so we can roast them and watch the sunset," he smiled.

"Okay," Bernard said, putting away the polishing cloth and the bottle of wax. "You stay here, Birdy," he told Senor Birdy, who was perched on the fencepost nearby. "You might get hurt."

"Awwk! I'll fly and meet you up there," Senor

Birdy squawked, then ruffled up his feathers, and took off, flying high into the sky.

"Silly Bird," Bernard said, then mounted Superbike and followed Turtle, Ernie, and Jojo as they all took off up the mountain path.

High above the valley floor was Eagle Rock, which overlooked the entire valley. From there you could see both Miners Oaks and Devlin Corners, and on a really clear night, even the lights of Flagstaff way off to the East. The boys all stopped, built a fire and roasted their marshmallows, then climbed up on the rocks of the cliff to watch the sun setting over the Purple Mountains. Senor Birdy soared in big circles high above them for a while, then when the boys moved to sit on the rocks, zoomed down and sat on Bernard's shoulder. Ernie looked over at Bernard and said, "You are a lucky guy, Bernard.

"Why?" Bernard said.

"Cause, you are the only one with a bird."

Bernard said, "Well, he's not really my bird. He belongs to my friend Hal, and I'm just keeping him until he gets back."

"When will that be?" Jojo asked.

"He didn't say."

"Awwk! He didn't say," Birdy squawked.

"You are still the luckiest guy in town," Turtle laughed. "Seems like that bird knows what he is saying, and he likes you too."

"Yes, he is a very smart bird," Bernard agreed.

"Awwk, smart bird," Birdy said.

"I guess I'm lucky too," Bernard said. "But I'm sad at the same time. I liked Hal, and he went away."

"You shouldn't be sad," Jojo quipped. "All the guys envy you."

"What for?" Bernard asked, amazed at that statement.

"Because you're the best player on the team. We never would have won without you. That should make you happy."

"I'm glad we won," Bernard said, "but I was just lucky. It was just a lucky shot."

"Seems like you are always lucky," Jojo said. "Kind of like you have some kind of a lucky charm, or a guardian angel on your shoulder, or something, and you are the best student at school too," Jojo said. "Seems like it's a little more than just luck."

"That's really nice of you guys to say that," Bernard said, bowing his head, embarrassed by their compliments. "But you guys are really the lucky ones, you know, not me."

"What makes you say that?" Ernie asked. "Why are we the lucky ones?"

"Because, you all have dads," Bernard said quietly, then he turned away, and a tear ran from his eye and down his cheek. There was a long silence when nobody spoke. Then, all of the boys moved to sit on the big rock beside Bernard, dangling their legs over the edge of the cliff, putting their arms around each other's shoulders, and they all sat silently and watched together as the glowing red ball of the Arizona sun set behind the Purple Mountains. The sky was pink for a short time, slowly turning to blue as a silvery moon rose to illuminate the entire valley, lake and mountains below.

JOIN THE SUPERBIKE FUN CLUB

Now, for the very first time ever, Bernard Wheel is personally inviting you to join the **Superbike Fun Club** so you can be the first in your neighborhood to get in on all the action, fun and adventure.

When you join, you get the **Superbike Fun Club** Membership Card with your name and address right on it for personal identification, a photo of the real Bernard Wheel and the Blue Angels, stickers, a letter from Bernard, and our special catalog showing all the great Superbike stuff, like T-shirts, Caps, and lots of other really exciting and wonderful things. As a Fun Club member, you will also be high up on our special list as one of the very first people to get a chance to own your very own copy of the brand new **Superbike Two Novel**, personally autographed by the author, David Allen Russell. Time is moving on, so don't wait. Fill in the order form below and Join us Now!

Send Cash, Check, or Money Order for only $3.00 To:

H. O. P. Inc.
412 N. Coast Hwy., #355
Laguna Beach, CA 92651

Yes, enclosed find $3.00, for my **Superbike Fun Club** membership card, letter from Bernard, stickers, and the super special **Superbike Catalog**. I understand that it could take up to six weeks for delivery, so please process my order as soon as possible.

Name____ Age_____

Address____

City_________________________ State_____ ZIP____________

Signed____
